Rean

"My my, will you look at the cottonwood blossom . . ."

"The what?"

"Somebody's had themselves a necktie party."

"Good Lord!"

Raider was listening, but with only half an ear, his eyes fixed on the tree ahead. A man was hanging from the lowest branch.

The hanged man was dressed to the nines, checkered silk vest, silk cravat. Raider surveyed the situation and, pulling his six gun, fired a single shot, parting the rope cleanly, tumbling the corpse in a heap . . .

J.D. HARDIN

BLOODY TIME IN BLACKTOWER

Ⓑ®

BERKLEY BOOKS, NEW YORK

BLOODY TIME IN BLACKTOWER

A Berkley Book / published by arrangement with
the author

PRINTING HISTORY
Berkley edition / August 1983

ISBN: 0-425-06331-3

A BERKLEY BOOK ® TM 757,375
Berkley Books are published by The Berkley Publishing Group,
200 Madison Avenue, New York, N.Y. 10016.
The name "BERKLEY" and the stylized "B" with design are trademarks
belonging to Berkley Publishing Corporation.

PRINTED IN THE UNITED STATES OF AMERICA

CHAPTER ONE

The earth lay like a dying animal, mutely groaning, quivering, slowly surrendering its will to survive under the fierce and relentless glare of the Kansas sun. The drought had persisted for seven weeks in Coffey County and in tiny Pole City, first stop over the border on the Kansas and Texas Railroad. The merciless tyrant heat held every living thing in subjugation. The residents moved about with deliberate slowness, sticking to the shade provided by the tall false fronts of the stores and other buildings lining the west side of Main Street. Stray dogs crawled under the sidewalks to escape the monster. Passing horses drank greedily of the hot water lowering in the public trough in front of Gatenbee's General Store, drank and sweat, sheeting their necks and flanks with perspiration. And helpless Pole City held its hot breath and waited for the rain to deliver it from its bondage. But no cloud, not even a wisp, a shred of cumulus showed on the horizon undulating before the eye; no breeze sprang up to bring even temporary respite; all indications were that it would never again rain in Pole City. Each succeeding day the heat grew more intense and oppressive, threatening to suffocate its victims, baking animate and inanimate alike, tarping the area with an invisible sheet of fire.

In a drably furnished, depressingly low-ceilinged little room on the second floor of the Meadowlark Hotel, situated across the street from the railroad station, two men sat, one on an iron bed which groaned resentfully every time he shifted his considerable bulk, the other on a straight-backed chair missing two back posts and given to teetering

1

every time he moved, one of its legs being slightly shorter than the other three. The man sitting on the bed mopped his ample brow with his sodden handkerchief. He wore his light brown hair plastered across his head, and he had a mustache that gave indication of lengthening to walrus size under his prominent nose. His failure to confine his mustache to an area bounded by the corners of his mouth was a mistake, reflected the other man, studying him out of the corner of his eye. Nature had already endowed him with a walruslike appearance: large and protruding eyes and a keglike head that joined his chest directly, without need for a neck in the manner of a walrus. Adding a full, flowing mustache to that face and bulk could not help but emphasize the similarity.

The eyes observing and the brain reaching this conclusion belonged to Doc Weatherbee, Pinkerton operative and occupant of the solitary chair offered by the room. In his lap sat his curly brim, pearl gray derby under the glare of his checkered silk vest and imported silk necktie, the knot impeccably fashioned and surmounting a stickpin featuring a single perfect pearl. His suit was likewise imported, tailored of diagonal fancy Irish linen, and his feet were encased in calf opera boots which gleamed like black mirrors. His appearance overall, so fastidious and immaculate was it, would have been perfect had it not been for his face. Ordinarily, he was quite handsome, his features well suited to one another and carefully, properly placed—his eyes sparkling, his smile ready and radiant when inspired to display itself. But today the left side of his face down to his jaw was concealed under a bandage that all but cut off the sight of his eye, while his opposite eye was swollen to closing and centered a setting of black and blue that suggested somebody's fist had made summary acquaintance with it.

William Pinkerton, eldest son of the founder and chief of the Pinkerton National Detective Agency, cleared his throat and reached for the washstand and the half-filled bottle of Frenchman's Whiskey and the tumbler beside it.

"You want a drink?"

"No, thank you."

"What do you suppose is delaying your partner?"

The questioner's tone was not solicitous. William Pinkerton's patience was running out almost as fast as the whiskey he was pouring into his glass. Sweat coursed down his pale face into the wilds of his mustache, becoming trapped by it, besoddening it, gradually rendering it as limp as a well-used bar rag. Doc himself was sweating, although he had had nothing to drink since his morning coffee. His shirt felt as if it were glued to him; his ribs ached; his eye ached; and the entire left side of his face felt as if it had gotten in the path of a well-slung 80-pound Vulcan anvil.

"He's at the vet's," he said. "He'll be along . . ."

The walrus gaped. "The veterinarian's?"

Doc nodded. "The local doctor doesn't fool around with teeth, and there is no dentist, so anytime anybody in Pole City gets a toothache, they get the vet."

The door creaked open. Raider came in glowering, one side of his upper lip stuffed with cotton, his right arm in a sling. He walked with a discernible limp. His dark glance, become even darker with fury, shot about the room.

"Where's a man supposed to sit?"

Pinkerton patted the bed beside him. Raider sat, keeping his distance.

"You okay?" Pinkerton asked.

Raider nodded. Doc noted that the response caused Pinkerton's face to fall slightly, as if in disappointment that Raider's survival seemed assured. Reaching into the inside pocket of his jacket, the mustachioed one drew out a neatly scissored newspaper clipping.

"You two rest your aches and pains a minute while I read you this. It's from the *Coffey County Gazette*." He cleared his throat, ran his index finger back and forth over his limp mustache, and began:

"Pinkerton Detectives in Brawl."

The abject disgust in his gravel voice rose to his eyes as

he raised them from the item and shot a withering glare first at Raider alongside him, then at Doc.

"'Two operatives employed by the well-known and highly esteemed Pinkerton National Detective Agency squared off in a fist fight last night in Gilhooley's Saloon on Blue Sky Street. Before the dust had settled the entire crowd joined in the hostilities. Michael A. J. Gilhooley, owner and chief bartender, has estimated the damage at eleven hundred dollars. The bar mirror, imported from Paris, France, and arrived and installed just last week after nearly six months in transit, was completely shattered. Gilhooley has placed a value of six hundred and fifty dollars on the mirror. Sheriff Tolliver has released both Pinkertons on payment of a bond by the agency's Chicago office. . . .'"

Again Pinkerton raised his eyes. "Need I go on? All right, who started it?"

Both pointed. "He did," they said simultaneously.

"All right, all right, all right, all right! *What* started it?"

"His horning in as usual," grumbled Raider. "What else? I was with this little gal, Edna . . ."

"Erna, stupid."

"Edna, wiseass!"

"All right, all right, all right, all right! Raider, you were with her and Weatherbee intruded . . ."

"That's the damned word, intruded. Stuck his nose in where it wasn't wanted. His nose and his big mouth with the fancy college words and his stinking frog perfume . . ."

"Eau de Cologne. *Avoir une Liaison*," snapped Doc.

"Whatever you call it it stinks to high heaven." His expression begged Pinkerton's sympathy. "He goddamn reeks all the time. Damned stuff makes me sick to my stomach."

"The ladies like it," said Doc airily. "Erna took pains to compliment me."

"Edna!"

"Erna!"

Up shot Pinkerton's hands. Doc noticed for the first

time that the man's thumbs were unusually large, as big as rubber crutch bottoms.

"Shut up! Okay, who started it and over what is water over the dam." Again he reached into his inside pocket, this time bringing out a crumpled telegram. "I got this from the chief. As I don't have to remind either of you, his health these days is rotten. He's still partially crippled from the stroke, his speech is still slurred, and when he gets upset he shakes all over. This disgusting exhibition has upset him tremendously. He sent me this wire. Three words. 'Break them up.' And that is precisely what I plan to do."

"See here," interposed Doc, "you're not serious. We just had a, what you might call, difference of opinion."

"*You* can call it that. I call it a brutal, barbaric, costly, and completely uncalled for performance that has not only rendered the two of you incapable of fulfilling your duties for now, but has blackened the eye that never sleeps."

Down fell the corners of Raider's mouth, and he nodded to Doc, an expression that clearly stated "not bad, not bad." Unhappily, Pinkerton had turned toward him as he finished speaking.

"You think it's funny, do you, you pea-brained saddle tramp!"

"Now just a damned minute, fatso . . ."

"No, you just a damned minute. My father, my brother Robert, I myself, and a hundred and fifty operatives and office help have worked like Trojans for years to gain and keep the respect of the public. The success of the agency is wholly dependent upon public respect, admiration, and trust. Now you two make the front pages of practically every newspaper in Kansas, brawling like a couple of drunken lumberjacks, destroying private property, endangering people's lives, all but braining each other over some dollar whore—and, as a result, deliberately destroy our precious image. Bastards! Firing is too goddamned good for you. If it was up to me I'd tie you together and horsewhip you to death. My father is on his last legs, and here you are, kicking him in the seat of the pants. And not the first time, although it's the first time you've gotten into print.''

''May I say something?'' asked Doc.

''Shut up and listen.'' Pinkerton paused, eyeing him fiercely. ''What do you want to say, you quit? Of course, take the coward's way out. How about you, plowboy?''

''Don't call me plowboy, fatso!''

''Don't call me fatso . . .''

''All right, all right, all right,'' burst out Doc.

''I said shut your mouth. Both of you. Raider, can you sit a horse?''

''Hell, yes.''

''Then do so. Pack your gear and ride out to Topeka.''

''What for?''

''There you will go directly to the railroad station and await the arrival of Inspector Algernon Braithwaite of the Metropolitan Police of London, better known to you two mongrels as Scotland Yard. Braithwaite is being sent to the United States by his superiors to study the agency's methods in the field. He will require a partner. Since you, Raider, no longer have a partner, you are to be it.''

''Oh for Christ's sake . . .''

Up arced Pinkerton's eyebrow. ''You disapprove?''

''How come I'm elected to wet-nurse some goddamn foreigner? Jesus Christ, it ain't fair!''

''It's fairer than you deserve. As for you, Weatherbee, you, too, get a new sidekick.''

''Anybody I know?''

''I doubt it, unless you're more closely acquainted with Bill Wagner in the Chicago office than I know of. Bill's sister, Gladys Hillbank's boy, has decided that he wants to be an operative. You will be his mentor. You will teach him procedures, you will imbue him with the ''General Principles,'' you will introduce him to every trick in the book. And if, at any time during your association, he incurs as much as a hangnail in action, you will answer to me. In short, you will protect him with your very life.''

''I'm looking forward to it.''

''Stop whining, you're both getting off a damned sight

easier than you deserve. As far as Mr. Gilhooley's bill is concerned, be prepared to contribute every penny due him out of your pockets. Fifty dollars a month will be deducted from your respective paychecks and paid directly to Mr. Gilhooley. At, I might add, five percent interest.''

"Five percent?'' snapped Raider. "That's road-agent robbery! That's—''

"That's the plan.''

Doc showed half a frown to the right of his bandage. "The damage was nothing like eleven hundred dollars. The man's a thief.''

Pinkerton ignored him. "Is everything clear in respect to the new arrangement? Excellent.'' He got up from the bed on the second try, pulling out his already soggy handkerchief and mopping his face. "Why don't I leave you two lovebirds alone so you can say your good-byes.''

"No need,'' snapped Raider.

Doc nodded. "We've got nothing to say to each other.''

"Parting company's the only thing I like about this,'' said Raider. "It'll be a pure relief knowing I don't have to rub elbows with him no more. Listen to his crap, his mewling, cover for him left and right . . .''

"That's a laugh,'' cut in Doc. "Hilarious. When did you ever have to cover for me in your life? For anybody? The whole world's been protecting you and pulling your chestnuts out of the fire ever since you were old enough to walk.''

"Kindly tell him to go fuck himself.''

Raider was on his feet and setting his course for the door. Seconds later he was out it, slamming it behind him.

"Eustace is waiting downstairs.''

Doc sighed.

"Come now,'' said Pinkerton, "aren't you being a little premature? How do you know you won't like the boy? How do you know he won't turn out a treasure? He may very well have the makings of a first-rate operative. You could wind up thanking me from the bottom of your heart.''

Stop talking, mused Doc. Shut up and let's get out of this shoe box and downstairs and the agony over with.

"Or started."
"How's that?"
"Nothing."

The lobby of the Meadowlark Hotel was busy with potted plants, overstuffed chairs, and the arrogant odor of old leather commingling with that of stogie smoke. Immediately the two of them entered the lobby, Doc spied Eustace Hillbank. He stood easily six foot four and his mail order black serge suit was a good two sizes too small for him, the trouser cuffs deserting his ankles for higher territory, revealing white socks. A single button on his jacket was hard at work holding together both sides, straining at its hole, threatening to pop. His jacket cuffs were also riding high, disclosing wrists the size of bricks attached to hands that looked capable of hammering home railroad spikes. His head was crowned by a wild-looking thatch of corn-yellow hair, and under it hung a face that struck Doc as close to the ugliest he had ever seen. It was exquisitely homely; Eustace, he thought, might better be walking around with a napkin draped over it. On second look only the mouth, fat-lipped and rounded, and the nose were responsible for the adverse impression. Eustace's nose was huge, the tip upraised revealing nostrils sufficiently large in diameter to accommodate his eyeballs.

They shook hands. Doc felt as if his fingers had suddenly become ensnared in a meat grinder, but Eustace's smile showed no malice. He patently didn't know his own strength.

Great God! thought Doc. Look at those shoulders. He could walk around town carrying a steer yokelike across them. Up close, shaking hands, he looked down on Doc from five inches higher. He lowered his outsized nostrils and wreathed his features with a smile, which softened and civilized them considerably. His voice was soft and pleasant and he had an eagerness about him, a gosh-all-hemlock naiveté and absence of maturity that was downright touching.

"I sure am pleased to meet you, sir," he said.
"You can call me Doc, Eustace. Everybody does."

"Are you a real doctor?" he asked wide-eyed.

"No," said Pinkerton. "It's just a nickname. He doesn't know any more about medicine than that stuffed perch on the wall over there. Weatherbee, I've got to be going. Frankly, I'm worried about Dad."

"Mmmm."

"I would think *you* might be."

"Oh, I am, I am. Please give him my best regards and hopes for a speedy recovery."

"I'll give him nothing from you, thank you. You've already given him all he can handle. Eustace, good-bye and good luck."

Off he strutted out the front door, vanishing around the corner.

"Well, yes," stammered Doc, clearly taken aback by Pinkerton's painful dart and momentarily caught off balance. "Have you got yourself a horse, Eustace? A gun, perhaps?"

"You betcha—a fine little roan."

Not too little, mused Doc, again studying his new partner's dimensions.

"Got me a Winchester repeating rifle and a Colt .45. Uncle Bill give me the Colt. Birthday present."

"So you just had a birthday?"

"Last week."

"And how old are you?"

"Eighteen."

Doc groaned inwardly. And mentally crossed his fingers, silently praying that if ever Eustace was called upon to use either weapon, he would not accidentally shoot himself. Or his new partner. For all his size and evident strength, the boy was outrageously awkward. His posture, his carriage, even the slightest movement gave it away. Awkwardness under fire could not help but slow one's reactions, and slowness, when it came to ducking, was an open invitation to a bed in the ground under a pine blanket.

"What case are we going to start out with?" asked Eustace.

"We haven't been assigned yet. But it'll come, later

today or first thing in the morning. Your Uncle Bill sends out our assignments.''

"You mean you and your old partner's. What was his name?''

"Raider.''

"You and him been together long?''

"Going on four years,'' said Doc wistfully, then caught himself, conscious of inadvertently betraying feelings better left unrevealed.

"Bet you had some close scrapes.''

"A few.''

"You got some beautiful shiner there.''

"I know.'' Doc investigated his black eye hesitantly. He then set about divesting himself of his bandage. He was relieved to note that the swelling on the other side of his face had reduced itself considerably. "Are you hungry, Eustace?'' What a question, he thought, as he asked it. Could anybody this big ever not be hungry?

"I could eat a horse.''

"I believe you.''

He walked Eustace out the door and down the street in the direction of the Pole City Restaurant. No breeze stirred the street dust, no dogs ventured forth from under the sidewalks, although no fewer than four pairs of eyes peered at them from across the way. Few people braved the street, a far larger number claiming the shadows on the opposite side. The level of water in the trough in front of Gatenbee's General Store was down to within an inch of the bottom. Glancing at it, for a split second Doc thought he saw tiny bubbles, simmering, but a second look dispelled the assumption. It was as stifling outside as it had been in the room, the air hot against the teeth, hot over the tongue on its way down into the lungs. Hot and excruciatingly dry, dry enough to crack the world.

He wondered how high the mercury had to rise before the blood in one's veins began bubbling. Raider was lucky. Covering the eighty-odd miles north to Topeka and his rendezvous with Algernon What's-his-name he'd be crossing the Marais des Cygnes River. It if hadn't dried up by now he could get himself a cooling wet, he and his mount.

He'd be well on his way by now. Everything he owned he could pack in his saddlebags. Gone, riding out of his life without even good-bye. Maybe good-byes weren't all that important, but there seemed something notably sad about missing this one, after nearly four years together. The argument over Erna was stupid, the fight that followed insane. They'd both had a tumbler too much. Raider couldn't hold his liquor; why he even bothered drinking was a mystery. One shot made him sick. As long as they'd known each other he'd had a weak stomach; half of what he ate he couldn't keep down. Strange, anybody that tough, that accustomed to a rough life, life on the trail with all the deprivations and inconveniences—the rotten food and rottener drink that go with the territory—should be queasy in the gut.

The bastard. He'd miss him; he did already. Missed their bickering, the fun he got out of baiting the plowboy, the Arkansas hay shoveler. Kidding him, putting him under the rug, especially in front of the girls. The insults, his vile temper, the way he got rattled when he couldn't think of what to come back with. His eternal cussing. Eternal threatening to quit, chuck it all and head for home. He never had, of course, never would, not even now. He'd taken a faceful from William, swallowed it bones and all, and ridden off to meet his new partner. What a laugh. If Raider couldn't stomach an educated easterner, a New Yorker with a B.A. degree, tailored clothes, expensive tastes, breeding, and *Avoir une Liaison*, how would he ever deal with an English gentleman, accent and all? Possibly even a monocle. Even worse, what if Algernon turned out to be a cockney? Either way he would love to be a fly on a Topeka station platform roof stanchion and see the one meet the other, hear each one's first words, their first difference of opinion, the first argument. Talk about priceless!

What was so funny? He had his own hands full. Oh yes, he'd miss Raider. God willing, Raider would miss him, too.

"I believe I could eat that horse raw," exclaimed Eustace, barging into his thoughts and hurrying his lengthy step. "I do believe!"

"Mmmmm."

Erna. On second thought, *was* that her name? Or was Raider right, was it Edna?

CHAPTER TWO

Raider arrived in Topeka early in the evening, weary, aching, and well dusted down despite a twenty-minute break taken on the banks of the Marais des Cygnes. He had divested himself of his sling, entrusting his dislocated shoulder to the care and keeping of the ascending spica bandage applied by the Pole City vet. He had then stripped to the waist and soaked his upper body in the muddy water, exchanging his sweat for the river's silt. Then he dried off, put his dirty shirt back on, washed down his mount, forded the river, and continued on.

He waited three hours at the railroad station, silently and not so silently fuming at this latest turn in his fortunes. While he pondered the injustice of it all, two trains came in. However, none of the passengers who got off lingered on the platform. According to the stationmaster, a doughty, red-faced little man built around an enormous belly, the last train through was scheduled to arrive at 11:45 that night. Raider's response to this intelligence was a string of vile language. He was damned if he was going to hang around that late. Stabling his horse, he checked into a room in the Topeka House. First thing he did was take a plunge bath half-filled with cold water, setting about scrubbing off the trail grime with an Alligator stove brush and yellow bar soap provided him by the desk clerk.

His room was only slightly larger than the one he and Doc had shared in the Meadowlark Hotel. This room did display wallpaper, an eye-punishing blizzard of white flowers with blood red centers that looked more like irritated

13

belly buttons than whatever the botanical term for the center of a flower happened to be.

Doc would know; the bastard knew everything, except when to keep his mouth shut. All the time blabbing all over creation, most especially when he could make this body look foolish in front of a woman. Bastard. He sure as hell wouldn't miss him. Fatso Billy should have busted them up ages ago. Would have been better all around. They were like a mule and a horse sharing the same wagon tongue; they just never had, never could work together. Not really. Still, they sure enough had themselves some frigging awesome times. Truly awesome; write home to the folks and picture their eyes bugging. Wild!

He lay on the bed naked, staring at the water-stained ceiling, which was cracked and starting to peel. He breathed deeply, sending discomfort lancing into his injured shoulder, setting him wincing. Doc had dislocated it with one punch, and it had been reset by that money-grubbing little vet with breath like rotten eggs and one eye that looked over your shoulder while the other fastened on you.

"Son of a bitch!"

Damn little curly wolf. Five dollars cash money to set a damn shoulder and another two to pull what was left of the tooth Doc had knocked free and stanch the damn bleeding out of the hole before he blood-swallowed himself sick to death.

Doc. Bastard. He looked so damn slight, misleadingly so, boy-sized in the company of man-sized men, but he sure enough packed some wallop. Lucky it was only a tooth and not his jaw he'd busted. He'd be wired up for soup for a month with a busted jaw.

Wiseass. If when *he'd* come back at him he'd hit him straight instead of glancing one off the side of his smirk, he would have stopped his clock for good, damn his hide!

He sure did plaster him with the granddaddy of all shiners, though; a beauty, big as a stove lid and painful as hornets. Had to be; the three of them sitting jawing in the room, every time Doc raised his voice, he winced. Good enough for him!

No, he wouldn't miss him; he'd be damned in hell if he would. Thank God the West was big enough so chances were they'd never again bump into each other. He sighed and drew a deep, deep breath, letting it out slowly, stretching gingerly, so as not to awaken pain in his shoulder again. What a purely pleasant prospect: never having to lay eyes on the overdressed, over-educated, undermanly son of a bitch again as long as they both lived. Undermanly? Probably was no such word. Even if there was, it didn't apply to Doc. He may have been a lot of things foul as mule dung, but he was all man. Give the devil his due; he sure proved his balls often enough when the lead flew and sang and rattled eardrums fit to split 'em. Come right down to it, old wiseass had more sand than a Cheyenne dog soldier.

And a hell of a lot more that was pestiferous about them than likeable or praiseworthy. No, by God, he'd sure as hell never miss him! Damned if he would.

He chuckled to himself. He sure wished he could see him now, without Doc seeing him seeing. Him and his new partner, Wagner's green-as-grass nephew. Big Deal Weatherbee saddled with a skim-milk punk kid. In two weeks it'd drive wiseass to the bottle, under the cork, down the neck and in.

"Oh, brother! Yeaaaaawhoooooo!"

A rapping on the wall beside the bed stiffened him in dire expectation.

"Hey, in there, would you mind lowering your voice?"

"Sorry."

"What was that?"

"*Sorry!*"

"I said would you mind holding it down!"

"I . . . yeah, yeah, yeah."

What time was it getting to be, he wondered. He never carried a watch. No need, with Doc handy, lugging that bull ball of his around. Must be getting past eight. His stomach rumbled quietly. Time for the nose bag, get a layer of beef down the bottom of his belly, a little some-

thing for the juices to work over. A thought came to him
as he got up and started getting dressed. Why not wander
back down to the station, look in on the stationmaster, and
tell him to keep an eye out for old Algernon? Buttonhole
him when he got off the train from Chicago, tell him that
Mr. Raider was waiting for him at the Topeka House.
Maybe slip red face and round belly fifty cents for his
trouble. He sure enough had to start watching his money,
what with the agency slicing fifty bucks a month out of his
paycheck from now on. Tight-fisted bastards! Allen P.
could fold a quarter he was so tight-fisted. Getting reim-
bursed for expenses after a case was like pulling teeth.

The hole in his mouth where his molar had been, now
wadded with cotton, suddenly felt sore as hell. Gingerly,
he removed the cotton, probing the excavation with the tip
of his tongue. The bleeding had stopped.

Tight-fisted bastards. Still, this mess of snakes wasn't
the agency's fault, wasn't Gilhooley's, either. Blame you-
know-who. Always horning in on something good, always
and forever sticking his nose in. Over-dudded pain in the
ass! Him and his wiseass mouth. What women saw in him
he sure enough couldn't see. A swallow-forkin' swivel
dude, that's what he was. Phonier than a riverboat jackleg
cheat!

"How charming; how dee-lightful to make your acquaintance, my dear."

Kissing a damn whore's hand like she was the Queen of
France. Bowing, scraping. Son of a bitch ought to be
dragged through a swamp and tuckered out in bib overalls
with no shirt and no shoes so's a female could see what he
was really like under all the powder and perfume and
flasharity.

He'd be goddamned if he'd miss him, the bastard.

"Bastard!"

He ate in the hotel dining room, steak and spuds with
the bark on. Jamoka. Sitting in a corner alone was a little
girl with tits the size of cantaloupes, but dressed for church,
all black with white lace chokered up to her chin, hair
pinned up. But man, what a blouseful! She caught him

staring and smiled and winked. He wiped his mouth with his napkin, slid a fifteen-cent tip under his coffee saucer, and left.

He went straight to the station. Nobody was around. The stationmaster's office was closed, locked up tight. It was two minutes past ten by the clock on the office wall over the desk, just barely visible in the feeble gleam of the night lantern.

Almost two hours before the train got in, providing that it came in on time. Even then it was less than likely that Algernon would be on board. Jesus, what a pain in the ass he was turning out to be already, and here they hadn't even met yet! Limey son of a bitch!

He sat down on an empty baggage cart and waited, dozing off, passing time half awake. His rumbling stomach kept him from dropping off completely, sending up sounds of protest against the steak lying at the bottom of it like a horseshoe in a bucket. Old beef, very old. Was it rotten, he wondered? It had had no taste, rotten or otherwise. And the coffee had been strong enough to float a six-gun. The world was going to hell in an ore cart, sure enough. Seemingly nobody around could make a decent cup of coffee anymore, coffee that tasted like coffee, flavorful going down the hatch.

"To hell with you, Algernon Braithwaite!"

He went back to the hotel. "Cantaloupes" was standing by the entrance, waiting for somebody. For him? Couldn't be. Still, she had smiled when she'd caught him gaping at her charms. Smiled and winked.

"Good evening," she murmured, smiling again, breaking into his ruminations on the subject.

"Evening." He touched the brim of his Stetson.

Good God, look at the size of that chest! If that ain't built-in back trouble for sure . . .

She drew closer, pushing her face up to within two inches of his. She smelled of lilac. Her eyes bored into his.

"I don't believe in beating about the bush, do you?"

"Huh?"

She thrust a key into his hand, closing his fingers over it. "Room 42. Come up in five minutes."

"Huh?"

Whirling about, she strode purposefully into the lobby. He followed her with his eyes as she mounted the stairs. He looked down at the key in his hand.

"What the hell."

As he opened the door, the smell of lilac struck him so powerfully he could almost feel his eyes water. A soft pink glow penetrated the gloom in the room. A Japanese screen was set up at the foot of the bed, with crooked little trees, bowed bridges and birds, and Japanese ladies walking around with parasols over their shoulders. He closed the door behind him, breathing deeply, the lilac scent suddenly acrid, lancing up his nostrils.

"Throw the bolt," she said behind the screen.

He did so. As he turned back to the screen, it fell over at his feet. She lay on the bed propped up on one elbow, completely naked, one foot raised, the great toe pointed. Slowly, she settled her foot and, spreading her legs, revealed her beautiful, jet black quim. Reaching around her enormous breasts, she seized it, pulling apart the lips, showing wet pink. Raider swallowed.

"This is for you. Can you fill it? Is that bump in your Levi's for real?"

Again he swallowed. He had seen forward women in his day, dirty-mouthed cock grabbers, women with two drinks in 'em that had to be all but tied down to keep 'em from attacking a man's sex-shooter, but this Miss Cantaloupes was in a class by herself. She clearly didn't give two hoots and a holler what she said or did or how. He stared transfixed as she began working her lips, her tongue falling out of her mouth and laving her lower lip sensually. He could feel himself starting to harden, his head straining his fly at the base rivet, threatening to snap it free.

"Come over here. . . . What did you say your name was?"

"O'Toole. John O'Toole."

"Over here."

He kicked off his boots, shed his denims, and all but ripped his shirt off on his way to the Great Divide and the twin peaks shadowing it. She covered her quim with one hand, demurely winking, grinning, rubbing it gently and sucking in her breath with a hissing sound. His cock twitched.

"It's hot, burning up. Come feel it."

He hesitated. She grabbed his hand and set it hard against her, lifting her hips slightly, pressing and rotating her quim, working it against his outstretched fingers. At the same time her other hand seized his cock, rapidly rising to erection, purpling at the head, becoming as stiff as a gun barrel. Her smile closed on it, her tongue whipping forth again, licking her full red lips. She began thrashing his head with her tongue, lashing it mercilessly, beating fire into it. Christ, muttered Raider, fearful that it couldn't stand the strain and, given thirty seconds more of this incredibly beautiful punishment, would split. Over the head came her lips, locking it securely, her tongue slipping, sliding, slapping away uncontrollably. Then she stopped abruptly. Winking at him, she began taking his cock, sliding the ring of her mouth up its considerable length to the root, driving his head deep down her throat. Down, down, down to hair and crotch. He eased one haunch down onto the bed, bracing himself with one hand, slipping the other around back of her head. Down to the base came her mouth, then started back up with agonizing slowness, gradually, deliberately, sending shivers racing up his spine and curling the hair at the nape of his neck. Up to the head, up, up and down once more, setting his cock gleaming, pulsing, throbbing, all but shattering like glass under the hammer of her brutal tongue. Then, suddenly, inexplicably, she jerked her mouth back up to his head and let go.

Instantly, she was down on his balls, filling her mouth, growling greedily, hungrily. He shot, come splattering between her breasts. Releasing his balls, she was down on his cock, catching the last few drops in her mouth, swallowing them, grinning. Licking her lips, she set about reworking his cock, restoring the hardness, refilling his aching, empty balls.

"Great day in the morning," he muttered and groaned aloud, a pathetic moaning that brought a smile of satisfaction to her face.

Again he attained erection and, mounting her, started his head in between her warm, wet lips. Grasping his cock, she hurried his entry. He raised his haunches and began driving home.

A sharp rapping sounded at the door.

"Myrna? Are you in there?" growled a voice.

"Myrna," burst another voice.

"We know you're in there," snapped a third.

Raider blanched and swallowed, freeing his cock, jumping up, detonating a small explosion of pain in his injured shoulder.

"Goddamn!"

Scrambling about on the floor, he retrieved his clothes.

"Myrna!"

"Myrna?"

"Open this door, you hear, daughter?"

"Who the hell?" began Raider.

"It's nobody. Pay no mind."

"Daughter?"

"That's just my daddy. And my brother Bert. And Earl, my husband."

"Husband?"

He had his clothes on, his belt buckled, his fly wide and his shirt as well, one boot on, toeing his way into the other. He glanced about like a cornered fox.

"Myrna!"

Thump. A shoulder against the door. He turned to look. A second thump, bending the panel. A hand rattled the knob.

"Open this door afore we bash it in."

He rushed to the window, lifting it wide, squinting out into the darkness. It overlooked an alley four stories down, black and yawning and likely brick or stone at the bottom. He got up on the sill with his legs out.

"Shut it after I get out," he rasped hollowly. "And pull down the shade."

She nodded, grinning. What in God's name was so funny, he wondered. The attack on the door persisted, the voices becoming louder. Damned fools, he thought, they'll wake the whole friggin' hotel!

Outside, he let himself down slowly, carefully, turning and resting the elbow of his uninjured arm on the sill and digging with his toes for purchase and additional support. But the outside of the building was clapboard, with no place anywhere to dig in. By now, she had opened the hall door and the three had come in. Everybody was talking at once, the men remonstrating with her. She giggled and laughed and Earl whined and carried on in a hurt tone, calling her "Myrna sweetie," and "honey pot." Damned if all three of them didn't appear to be afraid of her, thought Raider, cocking his ear to the conversation.

Time dragged by; every ten seconds his body seemed to add five additional pounds of dead weight. He couldn't begin to guess how long he'd be able to hang on. Placing the flat of his other hand on the narrow sill, he attempted to ease the strain on his forearm, but his injured shoulder could not take the pressure. The pain returning was agonizing, like a bullet piercing the flesh, finding bone and shattering it. He began sweating profusely.

And his left shoulder began aching with the strain of supporting him. Again he booted the clapboarding, looking in vain for a toehold. One boot slipped loose and dropped off, thudding to rest in the alley below.

"Goddamn son of a bitch!"

He loosed the other boot and down it dropped. What the hell good was one stinking boot. Nothing but useless weight. Inside, the four continued berating each other, Bert and Earl, brother and husband arguing heatedly.

"Girl's got a right to earn her an extry dollar, Earl."

"Not my wife don't!"

Raider glanced down into the darkness. Four stories

straight down—sixty, seventy feet, at least. If he fell he'd break both legs and reduce his groin bones to gravel, sure as hell. The window of the room below was well out of reach. At that, even if he could touch it with his toes, what good would that do him?

The four inside were beginning to quiet down. It was a miracle they hadn't awakened the entire floor. His arm was beginning to feel as if any second now it would break off at the elbow, tear loose the flesh and send him plunging into the alley. Closing his eyes, he pictured his forearm, hand, bloody stump and all resting on the sill and his corpse sprawled out in the alley. His heart quickened. The men were leaving, taking Myrna with them. He waited, holding his breath, fighting the mounting pain in his arm and shoulder. Finally, at long last, he heard the door close.

Silence. Reaching up with his free hand, he flattened his palm against the glass and eased open the window, up, up, all the way. He tried to lift upward, but all the strength was gone out of his supporting arm; gritting his teeth, he reached over the sill with his free hand and caught hold. Then he followed with his other arm. In the split second before he was able to catch hold with it, with his entire weight briefly supported by his stricken arm, the pain returned with a vengeance, shooting through his shoulder. He nearly passed out. Why the changeover failed to dislocate it a second time was more than he could fathom.

With an effort born of sheer desperation and abject fear of plunging to his death, he managed to pull himself up over the sill, dropping down onto the floor, panting hoarsely, striving to catch his breath.

A knock.

He stiffened and stifled a groan. Up on his knees, he rubbed his aching shoulder, rose to his feet, and sat down on the bed. Again the knock sounded.

"Mr. O'Toole? Are you in there?"

"Yeah."

The clerk stood in the doorway, smiling through three holes where there should have been teeth. His glasses slipped another quarter inch down his nose as he studied Raider over them.

"Had a hunch you were in here. Myrna asked me who you were after you came out of the dining room. I figured she'd make connections with you. When I didn't find you in your own room . . ." He shrugged and grinned again. Then he sobered, pushing his glasses back up into place. "You look in pain, mister. Anything I can do for you?"

"You can. Pick up my boots down in the alley, will you? They sort of fell out the window."

"Sure. You going back down to your room?"

"If I can make it. Where'd your friend Myrna get to, her and her brood?"

"Long gone. They're all the time coming to fetch her—father, brother, husband."

"Jesus, she must be some handful."

"One big happy family. Oh say, I almost forgot, you got a visitor. He's waiting down in your room."

"A Mr. Braithwaite?"

The clerk nodded. He left, and Raider followed him out, slinking down the hallway, down the stairs two flights to his room. Grasping the knob and looking both ways, more out of habit of caution than any real concern over being seen, he opened the door.

He took one look, swallowed, and rolled his eyes ceilingward. Seated in the chair in the corner reading a newspaper was Algernon Braithwaite, clad head to foot in shiny new leather, boots, chaps, cowhide vest, leather cuffs and gloves. The last he began to remove with the affected dexterity of a three-card monte dealer, at the same time getting up from his chair.

"Mr. Raider, I believe. How do you do. Well, I trust. Braithwaite's the name. Algernon Gerald Braithwaite. Just arrived from Chicago. I daresay it's a bit late, and for that I most earnestly apologize. I had originally planned to leave Chicago night before last, doze away the trip, and arrive bright and early this morning, but Mr. Wagner insisted I stay over and have dinner with him, Mrs. Wagner, and Mr. Pinkerton. Such a perfectly delightful woman,

Mrs. Wagner; she put me in mind of my maiden aunt Tabitha of Windward Cottage, Wessex. Utterly charming.''

He paused. Raider stared at him glassy-eyed.

"I say, old chap, are you feeling quite up to snuff?''

"Huh?''

"Are you all right?''

"Oh yeah, yeah.''

They shook hands. Algernon's watery, cornflower blue eyes fell to Raider's feet. When they came up again, they were questioning.

"My boots fell out the window.''

"Oh?''

Raider tilted his head to one side and appraised the Englishman. "You sure are all decked out.''

"To the proverbial T.''

"I take it you like leather.''

"Well, you know, when in Rome . . .''

"This here's Topeka.''

"Come, come, old chap, don't be so literal. What I mean is now that I'm in the colonies I intend to attire my person in the manner of the colonists.'' He slapped his knee and convulsed with laughter, a shrill cackling that set Raider's teeth on edge. "I say, that's a good one, isn't it? Colonies, colonists . . .''

Slight, but recognizable nausea gathered in the pit of Raider's stomach. Meet Algernon Gerald Braithwaite, Scotland Yard's best, he mused. Sweet Jesus, a walking talking machine, a living, breathing advertisement for a leather shop, stinking up the room like a damned tannery, Aunt Tabitha, a laugh like an addlepated ore-cart jackass. Billy Pinkerton, what the hell did I ever do to you?

"Now then, Mr. Raider . . .'' He paused. "By the by, is that your first name or last?''

"Both, either. Take your choice.''

"Raider it is, then. I was about to say, my trunk is below stairs. Would you be so gracious as to help me fetch it up? My room is just down the way two doors.''

A knock and the door opened. It was the clerk. Nodding

to Raider, he set the boots inside the door and withdrew. Raider sat down and put them on.

"I say, you don't think this outfit is a bit much, do you? I shouldn't want to attract undue attention."

"It's no worse than walking around with a lit candle in your nose."

Again the cackle; again Raider's teeth on edge.

"Oh, Jesus!"

Together, they carried the trunk up the stairs to Algernon's room. It must have weighed four hundred pounds, reflected Raider wearily.

"What the hell you got in here, lead ingots?" he asked, setting his end down outside the door. Algernon did the same and, inserting his key in the lock, twisted it and opened the door.

"Everything I brought. Better a trunk than four or five individual pieces, eh what?"

"You're not figuring to lug this monster all over creation with you, are you?"

"Why not?"

"How, tied to your horse's rump?"

"Surely, you don't get about by horse. Not everywhere."

"Just about. We'll be going places where folks have never seen a railroad. You'll only be able to carry what fits in your saddlebags and bedroll."

"Bedroll?"

They carried the trunk inside.

"Tarpaulin," said Raider. "About half the size of this floor. It's made of number eight white duck. Waterproof. Fitted with rings and snaps so's you can pull the flap over and fasten it. *Soogans* come with it."

"Soo . . .?"

"Heavy quilts, couple of blankets, and your war bag. It's to carry all your useless ditties and dofunnies. You know, makin's and cigarette papers if you smoke, extra cinch or bit, extra spur, whang leather. Lots of things. Bedroll's the second best friend a man's got on the trail, after his six-gun. You can sleep dry in the heaviest rain."

"My word. I can see I have a great deal to learn over

and above your methods and procedures." He produced a little black book and wrote in it, "Bedroll . . . *soogans*."

"But first off, I shall have to buy a horse."

"First thing in the morning." Raider yawned. "Now, if you'll excuse me, it's been a hard night." He thrust forth his hand. "Pleased to meet you, partner. Welcome to hard living and harder times."

"It's a pleasure to be here."

Raider returned to his room, fell on the bed with his clothes and boots on, and was asleep in three seconds.

The next morning, having taken a hint from Raider's reaction to his all-leather-but-the-buckle attire, Algernon saw fit to change into jodhpurs, knee-high boots, wool riding jacket, and a derby, in insolent defiance of the heat. It was a marked change from his all-leather outfit, but whether or not it represented an improvement was questionable. At Hilgan's Stable and Blacksmith Shop, around the corner from the Topeka House, he and Raider set about examining horses with an eye to purchasing one. An Appaloosa caught Algernon's attention almost immediately.

"What an attractive creature!"

"A mite too attractive, wouldn't you say?" asked Raider.

The Appaloosa pawed the ground, proudly displaying the color spots on its rump, its overly white eyes, and its pink nose.

"I don't follow you, old boy."

"Well, old boy, what I'm getting at is anybody with half a good eye can spot this pretty a mile away. In our line a horse is supposed to be what you call inconspic . . . spic . . ."

"Ahem. I believe I gather your drift."

The words came out tersely. Algernon plainly felt embarrassment in front of the stableman, standing skinny as a fence post, chewing a wad of burley so big it threatened to burst through his cheek. Shifting it to the other cheek, he let fly a stream of juice, browning the hay between Raider's feet.

"You'd like to peddle this horse, wouldn't you, mister?" asked Raider in annoyance.

"I . . ."

"Why don't you try the circus? Let's have a look at that blood bay over there, the one with the apron face."

They stood on either side of the horse; Raider checked its teeth, ran a hand down its chest, and cocked his ear at its nostrils.

"Magnificent beast," said Algernon.

"Good-looking, all right," said Raider, turning and staring at the stableman. "Though she sounds a little broken-winded."

"The hell she is," snorted the man. "Sound as a silver dollar. You should be so healthy, friend."

"I'll bet *you* a silver dollar she's got a bug in her lungs." Raider glanced at Algernon. "Horses with busted wind have a hard time breathing, especially after you've run 'em into a lather. Show us what else you've got, friend."

Algernon finally decided on a chestnut, a feisty, broad-rumped mare, all snorting and pawing and tossing mane. The stableman led the horse outside and Algernon paid him, peeling a sheaf of brand-new bills off a roll that would choke his purchase. Raider looked on goggle-eyed.

"How's about a saddle?" asked the man, licking his thumb, ejecting another mouthful of juice, and recounting the money.

"Man's right," said Raider. "You're going to need leather."

"Step this way, gents. We got a Texas saddle with oversized horn, steam-bent wood stirrups, lots more stronger than hollowed out, you betcha. Got us a slightly used Denver saddle, big and comfortable as a rocking chair."

"Too big," said Raider. "Too heavy, too long." He turned to Algernon. "A Denver tends to rub an animal's back full of sores."

"Got a California. Ten pounds lighter than the Denver. Fancy leather tooling . . ."

"Do you by chance have an English saddle?" asked Algernon.

"English?" The stableman stared with a puzzled expression at Raider.

"What's that?" asked Raider.

Algernon drew his breath in through his nostrils, his thin lips clamped tightly together, lending him a look of abject disdain.

"English saddles are used by Englishmen on English horses," he responded haughtily. "I would prefer one."

"Okay, but don't you want to at least look at the others?"

"To what end, old boy? I know what I want, and there seems little point in wasting time looking at what I don't want. Thank you, sir, our business is concluded."

Tipping his derby, Algernon started off with his horse in tow. Sighing, Raider gave chase, catching up and walking beside him, realizing for the first time that Algernon towered over his six feet even by at least five inches. And he wasn't skinny like the stableman. And his hands looked like a stevedore's—big, heavily knuckled, powerfully sinewed. These reflections coursed through Raider's mind at this particular juncture only because Algernon was beginning to show an obstinancy that could conceivably lead to a falling out between them. Since argument frequently degenerates into punching, kneeing, throttling, biting, and other methods of inflicting pain on one's adversary, it made sense for Raider to measure the man.

So he was turning out a stubborn mule, was he? Well, like it or not, they were a team, at least for the time being, and seeing as he was the experienced half, the last word would be his, in action or out of it. He began mentally listing the possible sources of friction: English saddle, trunk full of junk, firearms: Algernon had already shown him his pride and joy, a .32-caliber pearl-handled Dutchman's peashooter, a Mauser or Hauser, something German and even less powerful than Doc's .38 Diamondback. Then there was the man's clothes, his continual reference to old boy, old chap, old fellow, and sixty-seven other sore points. The storm clouds appeared to be gathering.

They got back to the hotel. Algernon left him at the front door to go searching for an English saddle. Raider tried to tell him that no such equipment could be found in Topeka—or for that matter anywhere in Kansas, anywhere west of the Mississippi—but Algernon refused to listen.

He tied Algernon's horse out back with his own. The desk clerk had a telegram for Mr. O'Toole. From Wagner in Chicago. Consulting his issue book, he decoded it. Some nameless troublemaker was riding around the Oklahoma Panhandle poisoning stock—entire herds—with the probable intention of driving up the price of beef. Local lawmen were unable to keep up with the poisoner. He was striking all over with the swiftness of heat lightning in July.

When Algernon came back an hour later toting a curious-looking saddle over his shoulder and clutching a riding crop in the other hand, Raider, sitting in the lobby, encoding his answer to Wagner's telegram, took one look and all but dropped his lower jaw from its hinges.

"Where in hell did you find that?"

"In a shop, naturally. A beauty, isn't it? Look closely, that's bloody craftsmanship, old boy."

"It's weird looking. You sure it's supposed to sit a man?"

"Quite sure."

"It's got no cantle to speak of. Where's the horn? What in hell are you supposed to hang onto? How come only one cinch? If it snaps you've got no safety. You could go flying into a cactus patch clear up to your hips. I've never seen such a shallow seat. You might as well sit on a dinner plate. Looks uncomfortable as hell."

"Are you quite finished?"

"Algernon . . ."

"What have you done with the horses?"

"Out back."

"Come along."

"Let me just finish what I'm doing. I'll only be a—"

"I said come."

All eyes on him as the vanquished in the battle of wills, Raider hung his head and plodded along behind Algernon out the door, the tittering behind him tinging his ears pink. Let 'em laugh, he thought. It was still a single-cinch saddle, like a California rig, and, like it, downright dangerous in mountainous country. One cinch just doesn't hold on a steep downhill course.

You'll see, Mr. Choke-bored breeches and derby hat!

CHAPTER THREE

The forge of the sun hung just above the horizon line, its orange slowly deepening to blood red as it drew back the sweltering heat it had been pouring over the defenseless landscape all day long. Kansas lay like a long-suffering steer, deserted by herd and herders, helpless, defenseless, doomed to die. The few streams and fewer rivers lacing the land were rapidly drying up, the sun stealing their water faster than the springs that perennially fed them could replace the loss. The tall prairie grass, bending under its own weight—for there was no breeze—had long since surrendered its life juices to the withering heat. A match carelessly disposed of or lightning striking could conceivably blacken ten square miles of the yellow sea stretching in every direction as far as the eye could discern before the fire died. Along the river banks cottonwoods drooped like willows, their leaves, usually dark green above, were bleached as pale as their undersides.

Head down, eyes on the dusty, narrow road stretching before her, Judith ignored the heat and dryness, pulling the small covered wagon easily, its rear wheels half again the size of its front ones, a wooden sign fastened to its side: "Acme Overland Apothecary. If you're ill, if you ail, AOA will never fail." On the seat, holding the mule's reins, sat a gentleman in his thirties, derbied, spatted, and, between the two, handsomely attired in a well-tailored blue pin-check cotton coat and white trousers in open and resolute defiance of the heat. Beside him, stripped to the waist, sat his partner, his Winchester across his lap, a wisp of smoke curling lazily from its muzzle, sweat running down his face, down his arms and chest and detaching large and foul-smelling drops from his yellow-haired armpits.

Doc sniffed, made a face of displeasure, and turned his head, but he did not comment on Eustace's body odor. He did, however, tap the stock of the rifle and voice disapproval.

"Ammunition is precious, Eustace, you really shouldn't waste it pot-shotting jackrabbits."

" 'Sfun."

"So is masterbation, but that too is wasteful."

Again Doc averted his head in an effort to minimize the impact of the odor dispensed by Eustace's underarms, which odor the dispenser either was unaware of or so used to he could ignore it.

"Eustace?"

"Yeah?"

"Look back inside the wagon for a small crate with a diagonal blue band across it."

"Diagonal?"

"From one corner down to the other. Dr. Grogner's Double Sulphate of Aluminum and Potassium. Alum, to you."

"What's it for, Doc?"

"Just get it out, please."

Eustace fumbled among the boxes in the wagon bed: Sir James Creel's Celebrated Female Pills, Howe's Arabian Tonic, Jackson's Embrocation, pills and powders, nostrums and homeopathic medicines of every description calculated to cure every ill of man or beast. Eustace held up Dr. Grogner's small blue box triumphantly.

"Here we are."

"Good boy. Now, pick up your shirt, dry down your armpits. That's the boy. Now, take a pinch of the powder and dust yourself under each arm. Liberally, don't spare it." Eustace did so, his expression puzzled, pursing his fat-lipped little mouth and corrugating his forehead. "Very good. Now put the cover back on. Some future patient is going to get a little shorted, but better that than this, right?"

"Right."

Eustace didn't understand and showed it. Doc sighed to himself. The boy was big and strong, even-tempered; he smiled incessantly; he was eager, cooperative, sincere, and a dozen other laudable adjectives. He was also possessed of two left feet, slow of movement, slower of reaction, and the bone-stupidest human Doc had ever come up against. No brains, no education, no common sense. None of the three in any appreciable quantity. By his own admission, he had enjoyed four years in the third grade before abandoning school and formal education forever. His know-nothingness had two halves: ignorance and stupidity. In respect to the latter—as undeserving of respect as it may have been—he put on a continuing show of it in all its varied forms. Prior to leaving Pole City with Judith, Doc had persuaded him to take a bath. Eustace had immersed himself in a copper tub, lay back, wiggled his toes, soaked his hide, and suddenly realized that he'd left soap and brush on the table in the corner, well out of reach. Standing up and climbing out, he had drenched the floor. Returning to the tub with soap and brush, he had scrubbed himself down only to then discover that he had left the towel on the bed, also well out of reach. Once again he flooded the floor. When Doc came into the room he was joined almost immediately by the guest occupying the room below Eustace's. The man was livid with anger and loudly complaining about the waterfall descending from his ceiling.

Doc had been in Eustace's company now for six full days, and he had come to the conclusion that the boy was a total ignoramus, that some rare malady had effected a drastic chemical change in his body, coating his brain with a film which no impressions of any sort could penetrate. Dead from the neck up was the way Raider would have described Eustace Hillbank; so dumb he couldn't drive nails into a snowbank.

The situation worried Doc. Stupidity invariably breeds irresponsibility. They were a team; each would have to depend upon the other; but patently, Eustace could not be trusted with responsibility. That he meant well was inarguable; there wasn't a malicious or deceitful bone in his brawny body; but as a partner, particularly under fire, he could easily mess up. He could be expected to mess up. With dire consequences. Consequences Doc shuddered to think of. The irony of it was that William Pinkerton had warned him that no harm, regardless of how trifling the injury, should come to Nephew Eustace.

"What about harm to me?" Doc had burst out resentfully.

"What harm, Doc?"

"Nothing, just thinking out loud."

Eustace's sole redeeming feature, the only one Doc had been able to find so far, was his incredible shooting eye. He could put daylight through a jackrabbit's ears at 150 yards, firing from the moving wagon, bouncing, jouncing, and all. How he had ever learned to shoot so accurately was a mystery to Doc, but he hesitated to question him on the subject, deciding that it was a gift of nature: compensation for everything else she had withheld from him.

And damned if he wasn't a likable cuss: always cheerful, willing, friendly as a dog. If only there was a little fire in the mud between his ears.

Eustace had one other weakness, as if he needed another: He drank, outrageously. Doc had let him go off on his own the night before they left Pole City, and Eustace had come back at four in the morning, roaring drunk, singing at the top of his lungs, bouncing off the walls coming up the stairs and down the hall, waking everybody in the place. Doc had succeeded in settling the hell raised by his partner, and the entire hotel went back to sleep muttering. Three hours later Eustace had awakened, bright and chipper, with no semblance of a hangover, bursting with energy and ready to take on the day. At the time, Doc recalled cursing the unappreciated blessings of youth. From all appearances the boy was made of iron; at least his stomach was.

"Doc, how far to Baptist Wells?"

"About three hundred miles down the road. Down across the Oklahoma Panhandle, hello and good-bye to the north-easternmost tip of Texas, and over the border into New Mexico."

"Tell me what happened again, what our case is."

"Eustace, how could you possibly forget? This has got to be the most absurd and bizarre assignment the agency's ever been saddled with."

"I just forgot. It went out of my head."

Doc could think of six rejoinders to this assertion, but he saw nothing to be gained by hurting the boy's feelings.

"Somebody stole the bank down there, lock, stock and barrel, everything but the bricks: assets, records, furnishings, cages, even the vault door."

"Why would anybody want to steal a bank?"

"Most likely to set it up elsewhere."

"Where?"

Doc sighed. He had been sighing a great deal the past six days, far more than usual, more than he'd ever sighed working with Raider. In spite of himself, in spite of repeated firm denials to the contrary, he missed the plowboy. He set a match to an Old Virginia cheroot.

"Where did whoever steal the bank take it?" he asked his questioner. "Eustace, how could I possibly know that? It's the core of the case, obviously. Our assignment is to find the bank, restore it to its rightful owners, and apprehend those responsible. Actually, Pinkerton operatives rarely apprehend. We're not empowered to arrest people. What we generally do is turn suspects over to the local lawmen. They take it from there."

A white-sided jackrabbit caught up with them, thumping along on their right some forty yards away. Eustace levered a cartridge into the chamber of the Winchester and raised it. Doc stayed him.

"Leave him alone, Eustace. He doesn't need his ears perforated."

"How about if I tumble him? We could skin him and roast him for supper."

"We could, but we're not going to."

"What time is it, Doc?"

"Tuesday." He stared upward at the blue bowl of the sky and then at the lowering sun, fleetingly marveling at the ease with which it had transformed Kansas into a boiling cauldron and even now, departing, was leaving it uncomfortably hot. "Hours don't mean much on this long a road."

"How long before we get there?"

"In this heat? Ten days, give or take. If we don't run into anything to hold us up." He paused. "Oh, oh."

"What?"

Ahead of them a huge cloud of dust was rising, boiling forward, coming straight at them.

"Company."

"Indians?"

"Could be."

"Which tribe do you think?"

"Eustace, how can I possibly tell at this distance? I don't even know if it is Indians. It could be buffalo. It could be cattle, anything."

"It's Indians." Eustace tightened his grip on his rifle.

"Put that thing away."

"Are you serious?"

"Dead." Doc squinted, looking for a tear in the dust cloud. "It's Indians, all right. You show them that thing and they'll want it."

"Ha, you can bet they ain't going to get it!"

"You can bet they'll take it, although you may not see them, not lying face down in the dust with a bright red cap where your hair should be."

"I'm not afraid of no Indians."

"Any sensible man out here is; you'd better learn to be. Now put it away. Under the seat."

Eustace hesitated, then complied. The speedily advancing warriors were in clear sight now. Doc groaned. There had to be at least fifty, armed to the teeth, bodies painted red, even to their feathers and the single arrow thrust through their roach-cut hair. Naked to the waist, they wore neckbands and other ornaments, and painted on their shoulders were human hands. Again Doc groaned.

"Are they Pottawatomies, Wichitas, what?"

"I wish. They're Pawnees. All war paint, going to or coming from battle. Cross your fingers it's going to; if it's

coming from and they lost, we could be in for big trouble.''
Eustace reached down for the Winchester. "Leave it!''

"But . . .''

Doc pulled up and set the brake. "Eustace, listen to me.
Don't give me any arguments. Just do as I say. Don't open
your mouth. Don't make a move. No matter what they say
or do. Stay cool, stay calm, keep a friendly smile on your
face, give them anything they ask for, including your
rifle.''

"Like hell!''

"You do it! You just might live to tell of it.''

The Indians came riding up, jabbering excitedly. A
sub-chief confronted Doc.

"*Uiska. Am-tadda-piratoe. Uiska!*''

"What does he want, Doc?''

"Whiskey, what else? Get back in the wagon and dig
out all we've got. Make it fast.''

"You think we oughta?''

"Oh, my God, will you move!''

Eustace moved, but not fast enough for the Indians.
Two heeled their ponies past the wagon, dismounted, and,
climbing nimbly over the tailgate, began flinging boxes
and crates into the road.

"Hey, damn you, cut that out!'' burst out Eustace. "I'll
bust your damned—''

"Shut up!'' hissed Doc. "Leave them alone. Let them
dump everything; we can retrieve what they don't break.
Just sit back down.''

Eustace bristled, glaring at the sub-chief sitting his horse,
grinning like an idiot at the boy's frustration. The Indians
in the back set the wagon rocking as they went about their
search. Judith pawed the ground nervously, flicking her
ears and wide-eying the red strangers. Doc lay a restrain-
ing hand on Eustace's arm.

"Sit still and keep your mouth shut. If you don't care
about your own hide, think about mine.''

The searchers found the whiskey, all six bottles, and
other smaller bottles whose liquid contents resembled

whiskey. All the bottles were handed around, uncorked, and consumed. Doc noticed the smaller bottles.

"Great God!" he muttered.

"What is that stuff?" asked Eustace.

"Dr. Bowlman's Emetic. And the bigger bottle, the pint-size, is Handleman's Good Morning. It's a purgative."

"What's that mean?"

"It means they'll be vomiting and moving their bowels all over the landscape in about twenty minutes. A teaspoonful of each is enough to get results. Look at them, they're swigging themselves silly."

Emptying the bottles, the Indians flung them about, whooping and hollering. Those who had gotten hold of the whiskey were assuaging their thirsts and passing the bottles about. In less than three minutes every drop of everything had vanished down throats.

"*Aceebo, anacha.* More *uiska,*" demanded the sub-chief, narrowing his evil eyes and baring his rotten teeth. He glared fiercely at Eustace. Eustace glanced at Doc for help. Doc held up his hands, gesturing helplessness.

"All gone, Groinface."

Once more the two searchers climbed into the wagon. They tossed every box out the back in a vain quest for more whiskey. All they found in the process were more emetic and purgative. This was as speedily downed as that confiscated earlier. The sub-chief came closer to Doc, raising his tack-studded ancient Springfield and setting the muzzle against Doc's forehead.

"*Uiska!*"

"No more, no more, no more." Doc pantomimed "all out."

The Indian frowned, ruminated briefly, lowered his rifle, then restored it to Doc's forehead.

"Gun."

"Right. Eustace."

"No, Doc . . ."

"Hand it over and quick. And get out those two boxes of shells."

"Doc . . ."

"Do it, you idiot! Now!"

Eustace did it, albeit with undisguised reluctance. The sub-chief leered, lowered his weapon, and waved them on. Doc released the brake and slapped Judith's flanks lightly with the reins. Off she started.

"What about the medicines?" asked Eustace.

"Never mind the medicines."

Judith broke into a trot. Behind them they could hear the war party thunder away. Doc handed Eustace the reins. Swiveling about, he thrust his head up, sneaking a look. A second dust cloud was starting skyward; the rumble of hooves grew fainter and fainter.

"Okay, turn us around," he said. "Let's head back and pick up the pieces." Taking out his handkerchief, he wiped his brow and the lining of his hat. "That was too close."

"They got my Winchester," whined Eustace. "It's gone, ammunition and all. Handed over slick as you please. It's unfair; there oughta be a law! Doc . . ."

"Please. Just shut up and drive."

CHAPTER FOUR

Sheriff Woodrow Z. Langendorp, visible presence of law and order in Baptist Wells, was not a happy man. He was upset and unpleasant, deeply resenting the invasion of his domain by two Pinkertons. Their presence, as Doc pointed out to Eustace, announced to one and all that the sheriff and his deputies were incapable of solving the mystery of the vanishing bank and that outside help was needed. It was an uncomfortable situation and one which Doc had run into many times previously. Raider called it stepping on local toes. It was painful for those attached to the toes and embarrassing for those doing the stepping. Doc endeavored to calm the troubled waters. The four of them, adding Garth Freer, a wide-shouldered, red-haired, uncouth deputy whose capacity for behaving stupidly inspired comparison with that of Doc's partner, sat in Langendorp's dusty, untidy little office discussing the case.

"Ain't nothing you two can do we ain't done already," averred the sheriff airily.

"Sheriff's right," said Freer.

"We can devote full time to questioning people, moving around," said Doc hopefully. "I'm sure you have your hands full with other things."

Langendorp frowned. "Folks ain't going to appreciate strangers buttonholing 'em."

"It's their bank, Sheriff. Their money, gold, silver, valuable papers. Solving this thing is in everybody's interest."

"Humph."

"We don't want to take any more of your valuable time

than is necessary, but would it be all right if we checked back with you now and then? You can be of great help, I'm certain. We're always heavily dependent upon the help of local professionals like yourselves."

"You trying to butter me up, Weatherford?"

"Weatherbee. Not at all. Just politely requesting your cooperation, as it were."

"You'll git cooperation."

"You'll get it," said Freer.

"Just see you don't go running us down 'ahind our backs," added Langendorp. "We're proud o' our reputations. Ain't that so, Garth?"

"Definitely, Woody."

"And you've every right to be," said Doc.

"There you go, buttering me up again," said Langendorp testily.

Doc stood up. Eustace followed suit. Freer followed Eustace. Eustace towered over the deputy. Freer looked up at him enviously.

"We'll be on our way," said Doc. "Any suggestions? Dos and don'ts?"

"No, thank you." Langendorp stiffened. "We're out of it; it's your baby now."

"Wish us luck."

"Humph."

Outside, Baptist Wells gave no hint of the tragedy that had befallen it. People went about their business as they had in Pole City, which, with nine hundred residents, was twice the size of Baptist Wells. If anybody was feeling the pinch applied by the scapegallows responsible for emptying the bank, it was not immediately evident. The building stood three doors down the block on the corner, the last building on the street. There were no hotels, no boarding-houses, no private homes within a hundred yards of it, noted Doc.

"In the dead of night, with no moon and proper planning, any gang worth its salt could easily empty the place. I'm surprised they left the front doors."

"Where do we start?" asked Eustace.

Doc indicated the general store across the way. "We could use a rifle."

"You, too."

"I have a handgun; it's generally all I use."

"I sure need me another Winchester."

The purchase was made, the identical model, along with four boxes of cartridges to replace the two surrendered to the Indians. Outside in the street Eustace thumbed a cartridge into the chamber.

"What are you doing?" asked Doc apprehensively.

"Test-firing."

Before he could stop him, Eustace raised the rifle, aimed, and fired, mortally wounding a slate-gray catbird on the wing two hundred feet in the air, bringing down a flurry of feathers, a corpse, and sending everyone in the street scurrying into hiding.

."You damned fool!" yelled Doc.

Sheriff Langendorp came striding down the sidewalk, his six-guns bouncing off his hips. Freer followed.

"What the hell's going on?"

"Just test-firing my new Winchester," said Eustace proudly.

People emerged from their protective concealment, approaching the three of them, coming from all directions. Sizing up the situation, Langendorp was quick to take advantage of it.

"You do that once more," he bellowed, "and I'll toss you into a cell."

"Sorry, Sheriff," said Doc. "It won't happen again, I promise."

"See that it don't."

"See that it don't," echoed Freer, setting his hands on his guns.

Away they walked. The crowd broke up before it was half formed.

"Eustace," began Doc.

"What, Doc?"

"Never mind."

•   •   •

Uriah A. J.—for Andrew Jackson—Swinburne lived by
himself, a bachelor, confirmed and dedicated to the status,
in a little white clapboard house with a cottonwood shingle
roof and a tiny yard filled with masses of petunias,
marigolds, nasturtiums, and other flowers. His vocation
was the law; his avocation, watering his garden in defiance
of the drought and keeping the insects at bay with frequent
and liberal dustings of red pepper. Swinburne was pressing
sixty, ruggedly handsome, white-thatched, possessed of a
stentorian voice and a flair for making his every utterance
sound and look like his final address to the jury. Gesturing
melodramatically, he filled Doc and Eustace in on some of
the juicier aspects of the case. Other locals they had questioned appeared reluctant to speak; almost to a man, they
referred the two Pinkertons to "Lawyer Swinburne."

"There's more to this mess than hit and ride out. Lots
more. Those scoundrels knew what they were doing every
step of the way. They didn't even have to break in."

"You mean they had a key?"

Swinburne leaned over and flicked a bug off a flori-
bunda rose. "Exactly."

"How'd they get it?" asked Eustace.

"Good question. Strike's me the key's the key." Swinburne furrowed his brow and began rolling down his sleeves.
"My gracious, didn't Langendorp tell you anything?"

"As little as possible," said Doc.

"His nose is broken. Small man, tiny mind. Let me tell
you how practically everybody in town sees this thing,
even though they hesitate to say so because you two are
strangers. Then too, everybody's still in shock. Yes sir,
not only did they have a key, but their timing was perfect.
Six hours before they hit the place the Santa Fe Railroad
deposited a $90,000 payroll. Anyway, to begin with, Erland
Titus was president of the bank."

"That's who hired the agency, the Santa Fe. Excuse
me, did you say *was*?"

"He's long gone since the robbery. Which, of course,
makes everybody think he was in on it. Seems logical.

Where else would the thieves get the key? His high-tailing it out of here sure makes him *look* guilty.''

"Do you believe he is?"

"Frankly, I don't know. I do know he had his cross to bear. His wife left him a couple months back. Ran off with a drummer. At least he called himself a drummer. Tall, good-looking chap, dressed to the hilt. Come to think of it, he really was a drummer. Yard goods. Anyhow, Erland took it mighty hard. Moped around town with his tail between his legs. Quit attending church; deacon, too. Poor man just couldn't face people. Took to burying himself in his office at the bank, hardly showing his face one day to the next. Worshiped his wife, Ellie. Striking woman; natural blonde; a figure to knock your eye out. Erland was bright, hardworking, a devoted husband, straight as a die, but not exactly the type warm-blooded women fantasize about. Still, he played it square with Ellie. Until she walked.'' Swinburne paused and stared first at Doc, then Eustace, his gray eyes suffused with sympathy. "A body can hardly blame him for going off the deep end.''

An unwelcome, unpleasant suspicion assailed Doc. For all his intended candor and willingness to help, could it be that Swinburne's objectivity was becoming slightly sullied by his fondness for the absent banker, his sympathy for his plight?

"I take it the Tituses had no children."

"No relations at all, at least around these parts. Ellie may have back East.''

"Indulge me, Mr. Swinburne,'' said Doc. "Let me try to set this up. Titus's wife runs off, he takes it hard, can't go on without her. He's determined to win her back, only he doesn't have the money or the freedom, so he hires a bunch, works up a plan, and robs his own bank.''

"So everybody in town thinks.''

"What do you think?''

Swinburne grinned. "You already asked me that.''

"You said you don't know; you must have a feeling one way or the other.''

"He looks guilty as hell, skinning out like he did.''

"But if he stayed here wouldn't it all have been for nothing, assuming he was in on the robbery? He'd have his share of the money, of course, but that wouldn't bring his wife back. He must be out looking for her."

"No doubt about that. After she ran off, after he got over the initial shock he went to work with a will and a way to find out all he could about the drummer—I don't know his name, never did. I told you he sold yard goods, although while he was in town he seemed to spend most of his time in the Silver Spur. Played poker from morning till night. Some fellows talk a blue streak about themselves while they're playing cards. Erland questioned everybody in town about him—after he came out of hiding, that is. Some say he even got up what you might call a dossier on whatever his name is. He was bound and determined to track him down and get his Ellie back. Really believed he could. It became his passion. It consumed the poor fellow."

"Nobody we've talked to seems to have any idea where he's gone."

Swinburne shook his head, then he raised it, a knowing gleam coming into his eyes.

"You find the drummer, you'll find her, and Erland'll likely be somewhere close by."

"I agree." Doc stuck out his hand. "Mr. Swinburne, I appreciate this. You've been a great help. Just one more thing: I assume the bank's locked up."

"Has been ever since. There's a notice plastered on the door. Closed until further notice; signed by Governor Gidding." Once more Swinburne shook his head and clucked sadly. "Sorry, sorry business. A man's heart torn out of him, he works himself up to a frenzy of desperation, winds up jumping off the deep end. People are crazy. Nobody and nothing is half as hard on 'em as they are on themselves."

"True. Tell me, who else in town would have a key to the bank? Anybody?"

"Annie Paltz. She's worked there for years. She and her husband live up over Piper's General Store. Incidentally, you might talk to Wardell Piper. I think that drummer sold him his yard goods.''

''We've already talked. He didn't have much to say. Maybe we'll try him again. Oh, one other thing. Do you know where we might get a photograph of Erland Titus?''

''I've got one.'' Doc stared in disbelief. ''The story was in all the papers; I'm a save-all of newspapers. Come on inside.''

Annie Paltz was something less than the soul of cooperation. She summarily refused Doc's request to borrow the key, insisting he first get authorization from Langendorp. Doc had little stomach for another go-round with the sheriff. Politely, even graciously, he explained that the law had offered full cooperation in the matter. He switched on his charm. On and up to full power. It was useless. She refused to give in. She sat glaring at him stonily, her lips pressed tightly together, as if she were afraid something would slip out. Her parlor smelled of bacon; it was garishly furnished, over-furnished. Clearly, she was one of those people who was continually acquiring things: furniture, pictures, knickknacks, doodads, but could never bring herself to throw anything away. Shown into the parlor, Doc and Eustace had to pick their way to their chairs. Now, almost as soon as they'd arrived, she wanted them to leave. Her expression demanded it. Studying her, all Doc could think of was a giant clam slowly closing, clamping shut. Turning off the charm, he turned on a strictly business tone, as frosty as he could make it. Next would come threats, he mused.

''Mrs. Paltz, I'm sure you've heard of the Pinkerton National Detective Agency.''

''I 'spect I have.''

''Pinkerton operatives in the field are assigned a case. Our job is to solve that case. By whatever means possible, providing, of course, it's also legal. To do so, we need all the cooperation we can get from people. Now I can get a court order that will force you to hand over that key. If so ordered and you still refuse to cooperate, you can go to jail.'' He glanced about. ''I can't believe you'd willingly exchange these delightful surroundings for a cell.'' He sniffed. ''And your cooking for jail food. The food given prisoners is notoriously poor.''

''Woodrow Langendorp would never put me in jail. We go too far back.''

''Given a court order, he'd have no choice but to. If he didn't, the judge'd put *him* in jail. Now I could have that court order in my hand by nine o'clock tomorrow morning. Your willingness to obstruct justice is my guarantee I'll get it. And your guarantee that Baptist Wells will look on you as a laughingstock for playing the stubborn mule for no reason any sensible person can imagine. If you think withholding the key is some kind of proof of your loyalty to Erland Titus, you're sadly mistaken. Mr. Titus is a wanted man.'' Leaning forward, he pointed straight at her. She shrank back, her eyes widening. ''This is a criminal case, and at this moment, you are deliberately obstructing our investigation.''

He rose to his feet. ''You have ten seconds to produce that key!''

''I won't do it!''

''Give him the goddamn key!'' boomed a voice from the bedroom.

All three reacted, Mrs. Paltz all but jumping clear out of her rocker. Sighing heavily in capitulation, she crossed to a sadly distressed six-drawer maple sideboard and, producing a small key on a chain around her neck, opened the center drawer and brought out a key. She did not hand it to Doc; instead she set it on the sideboard. He retrieved it. She then sniffed, went to the door, opened it, and stood aside. She was furious, but she said nothing. However, she did slam the door as soon as they stepped over the sill.

The bank was picked clean. The thieves had even removed the tellers' cages, wooden wall housing and all. Doc and Eustace examined every inch of the place. They found nothing, not even the hint of a clue as to who was responsible. They examined the ground outside. Doc found a boot heel and nothing else. Eustace returned Annie Paltz's key. He and Doc sat at a corner table in the Silver Spur cudgeling their brains, struggling to devise some kind of plan that might possibly take them forward in the case. Doc cudgeled; Eustace sat sipping Valley Tan and listened. It was dinner time in Baptist Wells; few patrons were on hand. The two waitresses—a slender waif with a face that vaguely resembled that of a ferret, and an overweight cow with heavily powdered breasts squeezed into a cheap dress comprised of approximately a million sequins—sat playing cards near the piano. Two drinkers footed the brass at the bar. The bartender leaned against his cash register, his arms folded over his ample belly, chin on his chest, dozing, breathing stertoriously.

"Go easy on the stuff, Eustace. You drink it like it was sarsparilla. We've got our work cut out. Let's keep a clear head, shall we?"

As if clear or clouded made any difference to him, thought Doc ruefully, hauling out an Old Virginia cheroot and setting a match to it. Smoking helped him think, he thought. If only he had pieces enough to fit together into a worthwhile thought.

"I'm fine," growled Eustace. "Don't worry about me."

"I worry about the Tituses and that drummer." He snapped his fingers. "Eustace, finish your drink and get on over to the general store. Ask Mr. Piper the drummer's name. Write it down so you won't forget it on the way back."

"Okay."

He got heavily to his feet, nearly upsetting his chair, scraping the floor so loudly he woke the bartender and attracted the attention of the two waitresses. The waif smiled at Eustace and offered him an exaggerated come-on wink. But duty called, and he answered. Off he went, Doc shaking his head after him.

What good the drummer's name would do them wasn't immediately clear. More important at the moment was establishing where Erland Titus had gotten to. On second thought, the name could be of value; the drummer had to be employed by a supplier. Doc got up, tossed down a silver dollar, and hurried off, catching up with Eustace just as he was about to enter the store. Doc grabbed his arm from behind.

"Move."

Like every other general store Doc had seen up and down the territories, Wardell Piper's was stocked to serve every human need, every fancy, every whim. It was a cavernous repository of quiet activity, muted voices, the occasional ring of the cash register, and an onslaught of mingled familiar aromas—everything from coffee to cheeses to condiments and spices in abundant variety. Piper recognized them at once, nodding, dusting his bow tie with his paintbrush beard and motioning them to the privacy of a corner.

"Something else on you boys' minds?" he asked.

Doc's immediate impression was that since they had last talked, Piper had entertained second thoughts about "opening up" to the strangers in town. Perhaps, reflected Doc, he had decided that it was in his own best interests to cooperate. Perhaps he thought he might get his name in the papers once the case was solved.

If it ever was.

"We have just two questions, Mr. Piper: What was that yard goods drummer's name, and who did he work for?"

Piper paled perceptibly. He almost gasped. "You get your information real fast, don't you?"

"From one source or another," said Doc drily.

"His name's Lester Sutherland. He works for the Astoria Dry Goods Company in Kansas City. Us two been doing business for close to two years."

"So you know each other pretty well."

"I guess you'd say."

"What do you know about his relationship with Mrs. Titus?"

"Not a blamed thing. That's none o' my business. He'd have no call to tell me 'bout his private life, now would he?"

"Would he?"

"Nope."

"If you say so."

"I say so most em-phatic!"

"Do you have the street address of the company in Kansas City?"

Piper held up one finger and, moving back behind the counter, rang open his cash register. He brought out a bill and, returning, showed it to Doc. Taking out a pencil, Doc wrote on his cuff: 352 Independence, Kansas City, Missouri.

"Thank you, Mr. Piper."

Piper shifted his gaze, looking over Doc's shoulder and scowling. Doc turned. Eustace was sitting on a bicycle, making believe he was riding pell-mell, twisting the handlebars back and forth and hammering the bell.

"Get off that thing!" snapped Doc.

They left the store, hurrying toward the stable.

"What's happening, Doc?"

"I'll tell you what's happening, I'm getting ready to buy a crate, shove you into it, and ship you back to Chicago, C.O.D. And believe me, I'll do it if you don't start behaving yourself. Raising hell in hotels, shooting off your rifle in the middle of Main Street, playing with toys in the general store . . . You're eighteen, Eustace, isn't it time you started acting your age?"

"I didn't do nothing, not really."

"When we get to the stable I want you to hitch up Judith."

"Where we going? After Titus?"

"We're going a quarter of a mile out of town so we can hook up to the telegraph line in privacy. We've got to get in touch with your uncle. We need a complete rundown on this Lester Sutherland from the outfit he works for in Kansas City. Cross your fingers. We may get lucky."

CHAPTER FIVE

Six days after teaming up with Algernon Gerald Braithwaite, Raider was ready to explode.

"I'm full up to the roots with you," he muttered to himself as he sat on a stump watching his new associate poke through his trunk. He had adamantly insisted on bringing it along, standing it on end on his horse's rump and tying it about his chest just under his arms and around his waist. He looked ridiculous, thought Raider, but that didn't seem to bother him one whit. "The way he hangs onto it you'd think it was goddamn human and had a quim instead of a lock." Humming happily to himself, wholly oblivious of his critic, Algernon found what he was looking for—a rectangular box containing an assortment of chemicals and equipment with which to conduct tests. Preparing a hypodermic needle, he approached the dead steer lying on the ground nearby and, kneeling, probed with his fingers for the carotid artery, inserted the needle, and withdrew a quantity of blood.

"Now, let us see what we have here," he said.

"That there's blood. And here comes Oklahoma rain."

A large dust devil came dancing across Pony Creek straight toward them. Algernon turned his back, and Raider lowered his head, shielding his eyes with the brim of his Stetson. The dust whirled through, and Algernon resumed working. Fitting a glass slide into the clips of a microscope, he placed a single drop of the blood on it and studied it.

"Mmmm, mmmm, mmmm."

"Mmmm, mmmm, mmmm," mimicked Raider.

"Amazing invention, the microscope."

"Ain't it, though? I sure do treasure mine."

"So rudimentary in concept and yet so astonishingly revealing. To think the proper juxtaposition of lenses is all that's required to unlock the secrets of the universe."

"That's just what I always say."

"Raider, old chap, are you baiting me again? What is it this time, my predilection for scientific investigation or my trunk, which, had you any say in the matter, would now be reposing in storage. Come now, old boy, you can scarcely gainsay the fact that the trifling inconvenience of loading and unloading it is more than offset by the contribution of its contents to our investigation, presently and, I assure you, in future."

"You want to know what really gripes me, I mean plugs my craw with bile? It's the way you talk. How come you don't speak English?"

Algernon gasped. "I . . . don't . . . speak . . . English? Ahhhhhhhhhhhhhh. I understand, what you mean is, I don't speak American. I say thar, podner, I don' give two whoops an' a holler iffn you see me an' raise me or stan' plum' pat!" He threw back his head and guffawed. "Priceless! Absolutely!" Raider spat and looked away.

"Will you kindly finish up fiddle-fucking around with that thing and pack it up so's we can get outta here?" He scanned the sky. "It's starting to get dark. We still got to question Hansen, then ride on out to Eva."

"I won't be a trice. Come here."

"What for?"

"You really must see this."

Raider groaned, got to his feet, dusting off his seat, and peered through the microscope.

"That's blood?"

"Look closely."

"What in hell am I looking for?"

"Note the red blood cells. They're damaged. Unless I'm grossly mistaken, arsenic's the culprit. Ingested in even a small quantity it affects the red blood cells and kidneys. Death results from circulatory collapse, failure of the circulatory system to deliver sufficient blood to the tissues for their metabolic needs.''

"Oh for Chrissakes! You mean heart failure?''

"Precisely.''

"Then why don't you say heart failure?''

"Heart failure.''

"Thank you.''

"Or peripheral circulatory failure.''

"Algernon . . .'' He paused, biting his lip and shivering his head as if to clear it. "This here steer's been poisoned. All fifty-six in Hansen's herd are dead, every one poisoned, you can bet your hat. Probably their salt lick.''

"I'd say that's a logical assumption.''

"So we know what the poison is, now all we got to do is locate the poisoner. I say we get on the death trail and jump from one wiped-out herd to the next till we catch up with the bastard and collar him.''

"Wouldn't that be something of a Pyrrhic victory? Think about it. How much better if we could find some way of anticipating his moves, jump ahead of him, and stop him before he, as the penny dreadfuls put it, strikes again.''

"How you going to stop him if you don't know who he is, where he's at, or when he's going to get there?''

"We know where he's been.'' He gestured at the dead steer.

"So what. He's got to be long gone from this neck o' the woods.''

"Neck . . . of . . . the . . . woods.'' Whipping out a pad and pencil, Algernon wrote it down in his black book. "Extraordinary metaphor.''

"I always thought so.''

Raider walked over to his saddle and, poking in one of the bags, brought out a map. Unrolling it on the ground, he laid a rock on either side to keep it from closing. Small red crosses marked different locations scattered about the Panhandle.

"According to what information we got, he started here; moved north, here; back west, here; here, here, and here. Makes sort of a rough cluster, wouldn't you say?''

"Indeed it does. It's amazing. What on earth is his motive? Wanton slaughter?"

"That it is. I've seen herds winter-killed and nothing left for the owner but to skin 'em. Happens in blizzards and droughts, too. There was a big die-up in Texas couple years back. Like this here: outright killing, skinners killing for hides. For a while there was a regular skinning war. But whoever's doing this isn't touching the hides. Like you say, he's killing out o' pure orneriness."

"There has to be more to it than that. It looks to me as if he's taking vengeance against the owners. For some real or imagined offense."

"Hell, that's plain as your nose, for chrissakes. Which means instead o' scattering all over creation looking for him, we got to look inside their heads." Again his eyes went to the map. "Six crosses, six different owners. We got to get us a list of names from each one, people they had run-ins with over the years—you know, bad blood. Then we check all six lists and see which name shows up on each one. That'll be him. It's got to be. We're wasting time. Let's get back to Hansen's and pump him for his names."

He swept the landscape with a glance. Steer carcasses were scattered about. He looked down at the steer Algernon had taken the blood from; it's lips had a faint bluish tint.

"This guy I'd like to collar, Algernon, really. Robbing and rustling are bad. Gunning innocent people down is a lot worse. It deserves a rope. But wiping out a man's entire herd is in a class by itself. It hurts everybody: poor helpless critters, the man—it'll likely bankrupt Hansen. He's just a small operator. He'll have to start all over from scratch. It drives up the price o' beef hereabouts, which hurts folks in their pocketbooks. It's like a damned plague— starting out, spreading, infecting everybody. Let's mount up."

"Would you mind assisting me with my trunk?"

Raider sighed. "I guess. You know you'd be six times better off if you got yourself a couple outsized saddlebags."

In response Algernon put on his customary grimace of

disdain, a pained expression that, had Raider not been familiar with it, would ~~have~~ made him think the Englishman had just swallowed something that disagreed with him.

"Thank you," said Algernon. "I'm perfectly satisfied with the present arrangement."

"With the 'present arrangement' you can't move your horse faster than a canter 'thout upsetting the whole applecart."

Algernon smirked. "Don't you mean a dad-burned canter? May I ask you something somewhat personal? Where, pray tell, did you learn your English?"

"At my mother's knee."

"Not in school? Don't they have schools out here?"

"I went to the little red schoolhouse to the ripe old age o' ten. I learned me to read and write and cipher, then I quit and went to work."

"And here you are, a diamond in the rough."

"Something like that." Raider stared at him. "I expect you went to fifteen schools. Been through the whole shooting match, have you?"

"The usual, for boys from families at a, shall we say, respectable social level: Harrow, Magdalen College, Oxford. Pater wanted me to be a barrister, but I wanted action. I've always been infected with a positive passion for detection."

"Is that a fact?"

"Of course my education did give me a leg up when I applied for training with the Flying Squad. I confess I was bloody hungry."

Raider stared, mystified.

"Impatient. Eager to catch criminals. Most of my early assignments were rubbish. I had to scratch for work. But I did well, so well I worked my way up to inspector in virtually no time."

"Got any notches on that peashooter you're packing?"

"I've never killed a soul, thank you. We're not authorized to carry arms. On the advice of my superiors I purchased my Mauser in New York. When in Rome, you know."

"You saying Scotland Yard doesn't carry any weapons?

That's crazy. How do you make an arrest? How in hell do you defend yourselves?''

"We manage."

"It doesn't make sense. You're going to find it's a whole different game over here. If you want to live to tell of it, you pack a gun. More'n one, if you're smart."

"I know," said Algernon airily. "As I say, when in Rome . . ."

"How come you're all the time talking about Rome?"

"I mean that while I'm a visitor here it seems sensible that I adapt my conduct and my actions to your ways, primitive though they may be. I might even say barbaric. Of course if I continue to pursue this line you'll tell me if I don't like it here I can go back where I came from."

"You said it, I didn't."

"Let's understand one thing, old boy, I didn't volunteer for this assignment. Like Caesar's greatness, it was thrust upon me."

"While we're on the subject, suppose I thrust something else on you." Unbuckling his gunbelt, Raider proferred it. "Try this on. Try the iron; get yourself the heft of it."

Algernon held up both hands. "No, thank you. I already have an iron, as you call it. My peashooter."

"That's what it is, all right. Mister, you can't lame a damn gopher with lead that little. We're going after men. You're going to need a man-sized gun. We get to Eva, we're going to get you a rifle, too, the best, a Winchester .30-.30."

"No, we are not! No Colt guns, no Winchester guns, no argument."

Raider sighed. "There's no such thing as a 'Winchester gun,' damn it. A pistol's a gun. Only rifle that's a gun is a buffalo gun. Now you're in Rome don't go calling a rifle a gun. I'd prefer you didn't embarrass me in front o' strangers."

Out came Algernon's little black book. Mutely mouthing this intelligence, he scribbled it down.

"Whatever you call it, I don't need it, I don't want it, and I don't intend to acquire it."

"Have it your way, wiseass." Raider buckled his belt back on. "You probably can't even shoot a rifle. Never laid a hand on one in your life, have you?"

"On the contrary."

Algernon turned on his heel, strode to Raider's horse, and slipped his Winchester out of its boot. Cocking it, swinging about, he took quick aim at a fallen steer forty yards away and fired, raising a tiny puff of dust at the tip of one horn. Raider ran over and touched the horn with his finger. He whistled softly.

"Satisfied?" asked Algernon, coming up behind him.

"Was that a lucky shot?"

"Would you like a full-scale demonstration?"

"You shoot like that, how come you don't pack a rifle?"

"We've already been over that. Come along, old boy, Mr. Hansen's waiting."

Sven Hansen was understandably deep down in the dumps. He sat in his rocking chair on a round rag rug in the center of his parlor, bathed in the glow of an oil lamp, his glasses resting on his forehead, a sheaf of papers in his lap, a pencil in hand. A big man, round-bellied, round-faced, and jowly, his speech was softened with a slight Swedish accent.

Algernon filled him in on what he had discovered. Hansen sat listening, rocking slowly, alternately rounding his heavy lips and rubbing the tip of his tongue back and forth across the upper one.

"Fifty-six dead, four left. Wipes me out, you bet you."

"It was definitely arsenic," said Algernon.

"I could see it was poison, them being blue around the mouth the way they are. Doesn't matter much what kind of poison."

"Oh, but it does," said Algernon hastily. "Certainly as regards our investigation. Whoever did it obviously used a large quantity. He had to, you see, to ensure sufficient consumption. It had to be purchased. Whoever sold it to him would have a record of the sale."

"Where'd they pick it up?" asked Hansen, shifting his eyes to Raider, in effect dismissing Algernon. "Salt lick?" Raider nodded. "I figured. I sent some of the boys out with shovels to bury it. Talk about locking the barn door after the horse is stolen . . ." He shifted his weight in his chair, and his expression saddened. "I'm giving the survivors sack salt."

"We haven't checked the lick," said Raider, "but it sure looks like the culprit. Either it or your water. The lick'd be easier. He wouldn't need so much arsenic."

"We can test the pond before we go on to Eva," said Algernon.

Hansen shook his head. "Why bother?"

"We don't have to," said Raider. "If you could send a man over to the lick and bring back a chunk we could probably tell by tasting."

"We could that," said Hansen.

Algernon glanced reprovingly at Raider. "I also want to test the water in the pond."

"If he put it in the salt, why would he bother with the pond?"

"We should be thorough," said Algernon stiffly.

"Mr. Raider's right," said Hansen.

"We'll work it out," said Raider, his tone consciously solicitous. "Mr. Hansen, let me ask you a question. Have you any idea who might want to do this to you? Anybody you've tangled with recently, or even back a time?"

"You bet your boots," snapped Hansen, sitting up straight in his chair, his ice-blue eyes narrowing. "I know exactly."

"Who?" asked Algernon. He got out his book and pencil.

"Never you mind," responded Hansen. "I'll take care of him. Good care, the best. I'll fix his wagon so's it'll never turn another wheel!"

Algernon bristled. "See here, Hansen, we can't allow you to take matters into your own hands."

Up snapped the older man's head. "Can't you now? Is that a fact?"

"Other cattlemen have been victimized. No fewer than six herds have been decimated, as far as we know at the present time. The association has hired us to determine who's responsible and bring them to account. Now you will kindly cease procrastinating and wasting our time and give us the name—''

"You go to hell, Mr. hard-boiled hat and funny fat pants. Who do you think you're talking to, the cook's swamper?"

"Hansen, you're being childish and ridiculous! We are working on your behalf."

"Who asked you to? Not me."

"The Cattlemen's Association."

"Get outta here!"

Fire flew from Algernon's eyes. "I'm warning you, Hansen . . ."

Raider took Algernon by the arm. "Let's go."

"Not on your life. Not until he gives us the name. By the Lord Harry, I've never seen such arrogant obstinacy!"

Hansen started up from his chair, his face reddening, his teeth clenched. Raider pulled Algernon bodily to the door, whipped it open, and all but dragged him outside and down the steps.

"Jesus Christ Almighty, what in red hell's gotten into you?"

"Me? What about him? Obtuse, mulish ignoramus!"

"Lower your voice, will you? He'll be out here with a shotgun!"

He walked him to their waiting mounts. "You sure enough know how to handle strangers, Mr. Friendly Persuasion."

"The man's an idiot!"

"The man happens to be lower than a snake's gut. He's lost his herd, damn it. He's suffering. He's boiling mad. What he needs is gentling, not bawling out. There's more than one damn way to skin a cat. You don't just grab it round the neck, dig in, and rip. Where in hell do you get off calling him childish, ridiculous?"

Algernon stiffened and stared. "Are you saying he's not?"

"All I'm saying is . . . Oh hell, never mind. Next time,

damn it, you let me do the talking. Don't you know there's times you got to use a carrot with a mule?''

He thrust a hand into his saddlebag and brought out the map. "Take this and head on out for Eva."

"What are you going to do?" Algernon looked past him, eyeing the house suspiciously.

"I got me a fence to mend. Oh, and give me that little black book o' yours." Algernon hesitated, then did so, pressing his pencil between the pages. "Now get going, I'll catch up with you."

"Help me with my trunk."

Raider growled deep in his throat and threw up his hands. "You and your damn trunk. I'd like to toss a stick o' Red Star dynamite into it."

"You do that, Raider. You so much as open the lid and touch a single solitary thing and I shall thrash you within an inch of your life!"

"Please . . . You're getting me all trembling and sweaty with fear."

Two minutes later the trunk was in place on the horse's rump, Algernon mounted and bound to it and riding off at a brisk clip, as if to prove he could. Raider looked after him.

"Stupid asshole."

CHAPTER SIX

Over the next ten days they called on four of the other five cattlemen victimized by the poisoner. Their herds were much larger than Sven Hansen's, and the total of head lost amounted to more than 19,000. The idea of each rancher writing down the names of possible suspects proved useless. Beginning with the four names Raider was able to persuade Hansen to divulge when he went back to talk to him, none of them appeared on any of the subsequent lists. On all five lists, not a single name was duplicated.

The Pinkerton and the man from Scotland Yard were scrambling, "shooting in the dark," as Raider phrased it. The only bright side was the fact that, at least for the time being, the poisoner was resting from his labors. The only consistency in the pattern of the poisonings was the killer's use of arsenic. Trough water and salt licks were spiked with it.

The relentless heat wave that besieged Pole City was not confined there, nor even to Kansas. The Oklahoma Panhandle, known affectionately by those who occupied it as No-Man's-Land, felt to Raider like the very heart of the drought. Day after day as they journeyed westward, no clouds appeared in the hazy sky. As far as the eye could see, the prairies, in earlier summer green and lush with wildflowers, were now brown and parched. The searing winds withered the cedars in the sandhills and the cottonwoods along the feebly running streams. All creature life seemed to have taken cover from the heat, even the birds confining themselves to what little shade was available. The towering cliffs the two riders occasionally passed, the craggy spurs, and the deep-cut crevices appeared to crack and shrink in the heat. The land was carpeted inches thick with dust. Tantalizing mirages and whirlwinds like spinning phantoms danced in the distance and fattened into swirling, blinding clouds. Algernon likened the area through which they traveled to the pit and acknowledged that he was awed by it all. He was constantly thirsty. Most of this affliction was in his mind, Raider knew. Under such conditions one doesn't become nearly as thirsty when one puts it out of mind. Within twenty miles of Wealthy, a tiny settlement made up mostly of sod houses, where the sixth and last slain herd on their list was to be found, they passed a small creek, so small it didn't even show on Raider's map. It idled its way through the sand, glistening silver in the sun. Algernon untied himself from his trunk and practically hurled himself from his saddle. Raider followed him slowly, kneeling alongside the creek, letting his horse drink, drenching his own head and face and sipping a handful of water. Algernon drank greedily.

"Go easy, will you?" said Raider.

Algernon paid no attention. The water was warm. Raider glanced upward into the sandhills, looking for its source, then back down at Algernon, continuing to guzzle huge quantities of the water, so much so fast he was now out of breath. Straightening, he pulled the horse to the water's edge, and she drank slowly, just enough to wash the dust out of her throat, observed Raider. Algernon, meanwhile, was bent over and guzzling again.

"Algernon, I'm telling you, go easy. You're going to gyp yourself."

Algernon straightened a second time. "Gyp?" He frowned, puzzled. "Defraud . . .?"

"Hell no, I mean gypsum. Can't you taste it? This water's loaded with it. You can drink some, but too much in this heat, warm like it is, you'll get gut-twisted like you'd never believe possible. Ever eat too many green apples when you were a little tad?"

Algernon ignored him and returned to drinking. Finishing, wiping his mouth, he filled his canteen.

"I'll no doubt get cramps, but I've had them before and I shall have them again. Two Seidlitz powders will provide relief. I must confess, Raider, I have never in my entire life been so thirsty. It's a wonder my throat isn't cracked." He sighed contentedly. "It's not the tastiest water I've ever drunk, but it couldn't be timelier or more welcome."

"You're going to be gypped, you'll see. Don't crab to me when it hits and you start howling. Ever drink croton oil?"

"No."

"Me, either, but the old-timers say it's the same feeling—your guts get all knotted up, then explode. You feel like you want to lay down and die."

"My threshhold of pain is uncommonly high. Besides"—he smiled and patted his pocket—"there's always the Seidlitz powders."

They rode on. Every so often Raider would glance over at his companion. When the cramps began to take hold, his expression would change, he knew. Within twenty minutes it began to do so. He started out looking harried, as if some worry had leaped to mind; then his expression turned painful, then frightened. Within minutes, he was rubbing his lower belly with his free hand and breathing haltingly. He took two Seidlitz powders. Two minutes later he took two more. Their effect upon the gypsum cramps, concluded Raider, looking on wordlessly, was next to negligible, like spitting on a forest fire.

"Those powders really help, right?"

Algernon said nothing, continuing to suffer in silence. Suddenly, he pulled his horse up short, undid his trunk ropes, jumped from the saddle—hitting the ground simultaneously with his trunk—and dropped to his knees, gripping his stomach with both hands, grinding it, bending, straightening, bending, straightening, and bellowing like a mortally stricken bull.

"Great God in heaven! I'm dying, I'm dying, I'm dying! It's killing me!"

"I hate to say I told you so . . ."

"Do something, you idiot!"

"Like what? Wave my hand and make it go away?"

"Oh, dear God, dear God, dear God, dear God . . ."

"How's about another couple Seidlitz powders?"

Algernon glared at him fiercely, hatred firing his eyes, his lip curling in resentment. "Why didn't you stop me?" he gasped. "You knew . . ."

"I told you, didn't I?"

"Too late, damn you. You heartless swine! Ahhhh, ahhh, ahhhh! How long does it last?" Bending, straightening, bending, straightening, kneading his belly, moaning, groaning—the pain must have been excruciating.

"Give it a couple days, the worst'll be over."

"My God, I can't stand it, it's ripping my intestines to shreds."

"Feels that way, doesn't it? But it's really not. It's just kinda, what you might call, rearranging them."

"Oh, God!"

An hour later the worst was over. Two hours and twenty Seidlitz powders later the last vestige of pain had disappeared, leaving the patient shaken, chalk-faced, and bathed in sweat. They passed through a settlement that, like the offending creek, was not even on the map. They continued on about two miles when Raider slowed his horse and pointed ahead of them. Buzzards wheeled slowly above a lone cottonwood in the distance. But it was not at the tree that he pointed. A slender stream ventured close to the road, then strayed away into a thicket.

"Thirsty?" he asked.

Algernon flung his hand out, angrily dismissing him. "Foul, filthy country. Disgusting! The people living here have to be animals. They deserve their cattle poisoned."

"I don't think any man deserves that. You can't blame the people for the water."

"They're all cretins—either that or scoundrels hiding out."

Raider was listening, but with only half an ear. His eyes were fixed on the tree ahead. Closing on it gradually brought the hidden side into view. A man was hanging from the lowest branch.

"My my, will you look at the cottonwood blossom."

"The what?"

"Somebody's had themselves a necktie party."

"Good Lord!"

They picked up the pace. Raider pulled up first. The hanged man was dressed to the nines: checkered silk vest, silk cravat, expensive tailored suit, well-shined Bluchers; all that was missing appeared to be his hat. A breeze came up, swinging him slowly. Raider surveyed the situation and, pulling his six-gun, fired a single shot, parting the rope cleanly, tumbling the corpse in a heap.

"That was rather a crude way of bringing the poor chap down, I must say."

"I doubt he much cares. It's either that or cut down the tree. I sure don't see any ladder around. Let's look him over."

He knelt beside the corpse and began going through his pockets. Algernon, meanwhile, laid the back of his hand against one cheek.

"I'd say he hasn't been dead more than an hour or so. Poor chap, I wonder what he did to bring this down upon his head?"

Horses were approaching, two riders coming from the nameless settlement through which they had just passed. One wore a sheriff's badge; the other man, older than the lawman by a good ten years, concealed his face behind a heavy beard. The sheriff drew his gun.

"Just hold your horses there, fellows, and back away from him."

"We just got here ourselves, Sheriff," said Raider. "We didn't do it, if that's what you're thinking."

"Didn't say you did. It happens I know you didn't."

Raider had backed away as he was told. He was looking through the dead man's billfold. In it were $34 in greenbacks, some snapshots, assorted business cards, and six more, bearing the same name.

"Lester Sutherland," he read. "Astoria Dry Goods Company, 352 Independence, Kansas City, Missouri."

"Hand that over," snapped the sheriff.

"We were simply passing by, Sheriff," began Algernon tightly.

The sheriff ignored him, holstering his weapon and concentrating on the contents of the billfold.

"You'll have to forgive me, gents, this foolishness has got me a little upset. Who might you two be?"

"Mr. O'Toole and Mr. Hamilton," said Raider.

The older of the two newcomers responded, offering his hand. "I'm Hubert Strayhorn and this here's Sheriff Rowland."

"Pardon my curiosity," said Raider, "but would you mind telling us how this came about? Any ideas?"

"Lester Sutherland," said the sheriff, holding a card at arm's length, moving it slowly into focus. "He was a drummer, all right, Hubie. Tell these fellows what happened, what you told me." Rowland looked up from the card, restoring it to its pocket. "I was away from Glory on business all morning."

The older man nodded at the corpse. "He was playing poker at Cattle Annie's. I was at the bar. Four fellas come marching in covered with trail dust like they'd been riding for weeks. He, Sutherland, jumps up from the table and goes for his gun, but one of the four gets the drop on him and they march him out. Whilst they was mounting up, with him carrying on, protesting, demanding somebody get the sheriff here and give him protection, bellowing his lungs out, I overhear one o' the four tell the man next to me that this one shot a body in the back in cold blood over to Blacktower in New Mexico, a preacher no less. Then he lit out, and the four of 'em been on his trail ever since. Said they was taking him back to Blacktower to stand trial."

"Didn't get far before they changed their minds about that," said the sheriff dryly.

"Aren't too many preacher-shooters get to see the inside of a courtroom," said Raider.

"Amen to that," said the sheriff.

Raider exchanged glances with Algernon. "I guess we'll be on our way."

"Where to?"

"Clovis," said Raider hurriedly.

"Have yourselves a nice ride," said the sheriff. "Though I don't know how you can in this heat." He doffed his Stetson, wiped the sweat out of the lining, and mopped his forehead. Then he glanced upward at the buzzards circling. "Sorry to disappoint you two."

Raider and Algernon rode off.

"Hamilton?" asked Algernon. "Where did that name come from?"

"Same place I got Clovis, off the top o' my head." He glanced back. The sheriff and Strayhorn were laying the dead man over the sheriff's horse in front of his saddle. "Poor bastard," murmured Raider.

"If he killed a man of the cloth I'd say he got what he deserved."

"I don't care who he killed, what he deserves is a judge and jury, not four hotheads stringing him up." He sighed dejectedly. "Welcome to No-Man's-Land."

To Raider's gasping astonishment, upon arriving in Wealthy, Algernon's obstinacy abruptly gave way to a seizure of horse sense. From the rear, his mare looked suspiciously like a pack mule under the weight of the Englishman's new oversized saddlebags crammed with the contents of his trunk. Algernon steadfastly refused to acknowledge his change of heart, not even so much as a shrug of concession to show that he was giving in to his partner's suggestion, but Raider had no need for it. Getting rid of the trunk was all he wanted. In it was not only a slender copy of Allan Pinkerton's "General Principles," but a volume so thick, Raider needed both hands to pick it up. This was Algernon's issue copy of Scotland Yard's "General Orders." Why he bothered to bring it with him all the way from London was a mystery to Raider. It was, he told himself, about as necessary to their investigations as a bat in a mule's ear. It also added fifteen unneeded pounds to the weight of the trunk; he persuaded Algernon to mail it home.

In Wealthy, a town of approximately eight hundred

souls, and the center for boozing and brawling in the county, Raider again tried to talk Algernon into buying a Winchester. Algernon refused to so. On the sly, Raider bought a second one and two hundred cartridges for backup. He could ill afford the expense; what he could afford even less was the chance of being pinned down by miscreants and finding themselves with but one rifle with which to defend their hides.

T. Aubrey Soames's herd of four thousand Herefords had been decimated by the poisoner. They came upon Soames sitting on his front stoop, a half-emptied bottle of Taos Lightning sitting alongside him, his bald head in his hands, his pan-plain and hairless face wearing an expression so sorrowful Raider felt a distinct tug in his heart. The man was devastated; the wholesale annihilation of his cattle had, by his own admission, stunned him.

"When I got word, it was all I could do to keep from airing my paunch. You should have seen me, tears running down my cheeks, my heart pounding like a trip-hammer, my legs so watery weak I could hardly stand. For a time I couldn't catch my breath. I was just . . . just plumb crushed, that's the only word for it. It took me seven years to build my herd up, seven years' work, money, and dreams, bingo, right down the hole. It's enough to make a fellow fit his gun against his head. If you two catch who did this to me, promise me one thing. Promise me you won't kill him. What you do is bring him back here and let me peel his hide off, then bury him raw in the biggest anthill in the Panhandle. You know, Apache-style."

"We'll find him," said Raider determinedly, feeling Algernon's eyes boring into him as he spoke. He shouldn't be making any such promise out of hand. Up to now they hadn't the slightest lead, but Soames's eyes were begging him to say something optimistic, and he couldn't resist doing it.

"Why don't we start out with the obvious question," said Algernon. "Whom do you know who might have done this to you?"

Soames swigged, proferred the bottle, was declined, and

scratched his head as he plunged into thought. He then ticked four names off on his stubby fingers. Algernon wrote them down.

"That last, Jasper Wilke, was one sorry number. He raised the roof when Scanlan, that's my foreman, Pete Scanlan, gave him his walking papers."

"Why did he?" asked Raider.

"Man couldn't cut it. He was a little shrimp, half blind and with a badly bummed-up knee. Could hardly walk, and couldn't ride worth a lick. White-faced cattle aren't the easiest to herd. They're docile enough, but they spook easy, leastwise mine always seemed to. Boys had to bunch them tight. Once in a while it was necessary to rope a steer if he started acting up, sometimes a really big one. If he showed fight and was hard driving to the pen, he'd have to be thrown. Wilke wasn't pulling his weight and he knew it, and once when a big boy began stirring up a fuss, he volunteered to handle it. Wanted to prove himself in front of the other boys, you know. What he wound up doing was practically getting himself killed, crushed by that steer falling on him. He came out of it shaking in his boots and red as roses he was so embarrassed. Pete was honestly afraid he'd get himself killed, so he offered him a job as cook's swamper. Wilke turned him down cold. Wanted no part of anything except herding, and he was no good at all at it. So we had no choice, we finally let him go."

Algernon studied him. "You say he was small with poor eyesight and a crippled knee?"

"And not much good on a horse?" added Raider.

He and Algernon exchanged glances. Dawn came up on both their faces.

"Hobart!" burst Algernon.

"Right, and, and . . ."

Algernon flipped open his book. He riffled the pages. "Donaldson!"

Soames looked from one to the other mystified. "Mind telling me what you're talking about?"

"Mr. Soames," said Algernon, "we've been collecting names from all the cattlemen who have been victimized.

We've never seen the same name show up twice on any of the six different lists, including your own. But your description of—''

''—Jasper Wilke—''

''—fits two other names to a T,'' continued Raider. ''What threw us, what's been throwing us all along, is that shorty with the bad eyes *has been changing his name every time he gets cut loose.* Looks to me like he's been planning this mischief since back when.''

''At one time or another he must have been employed by all six ranchers,'' went on Algernon, ''under six different names. He was discharged, and now he's out taking vengeance.''

''The son of a bitch!''

''I'm going to ask you a stupid question,'' said Raider. ''Would you have the foggiest idea where the little bastard went to after you gave him his walking papers?''

Soames shook his head.

''How could he possibly know that?'' asked Algernon, his tone irritated.

''I said it was stupid, didn't I?'' mumbled Raider.

''Mr. Soames, what else can you tell us about Wilke?''

''Not much. Pete knew him a lot better than I did, working with him and all.'' His hand shot up. Raider and Algernon turned. A tall, swarthy man with a mean face shadowed with three days' beard came striding toward them in the company of two other hands. His face broke into a grin, erasing the meanness.

'' 'lo, T.A.''

''Pete, this here's Mr. Raider and Mr. Braithwaite of the Pinkerton Detective Agency. They're working on this thing for the Cattlemen's Association. They'd like a word with you about Jasper Wilke.''

Scanlan's eyebrow arched as he availed himself of the bottle on the stoop and took a generous swig.

''Runt o' the litter, that was Jasper. Everything about him was small, 'cept his mouth. Had a chip on his shoulder to boot. Never did tangle with anybody, though. Hell, anybody with one arm under ninety could have licked the

tar out of him. That was the strangest thing about him—
not his eyes or his game knee or that he was all the time
blaming his horse for his own messing up—oddest thing
was he wasn't anything like most little fellows with two
strikes against 'em. He wasn't eager, wasn't easy to get
along with, hardworking, you know, all the cards most
little fellows hold to make up for their lack o' size, muscle,
riding ability, and such like. He lasted what, T.A., about
three weeks with us?''

"Thereabouts.''

"Wasn't a man here wasn't glad to see him go.'' He
paused and swiveled his glance between Raider and
Algernon. "You think he did this to the herd?''

Algernon detailed the basis for the sudden promotion of
Jasper Wilke—Ames Hobart—Lafe Donaldson to the position of prime suspect.

"If we went back to the remaining three ranchers and
asked them about him, you can bet they'd fit his description to one of the names they gave us,'' said Raider.
"Still, there's no need to go back,'' he added, looking
toward Algernon. "Three out of the six is enough to
pinpoint him as worth going looking for.''

"Where?'' asked Scanlan.

Raider shrugged.

Algernon spoke up. "Mr. Soames, you can do something for us. Assemble all your men, all those who knew
Wilke, and let us question them. The chap was obviously a
drifter; it's doubtful he ever mentioned where he came
from, where his precious job was, but he may have di-
vulged where he came from originally. Or possibly where
he was going on to.''

How come, reflected Raider, that question is stupid
when I ask it and makes sense when you do? Maybe they
should talk about that, he thought, only another time and
place.

Soames called together his hands, and they did their best
to stir the coals of memory, but nobody could contribute
anything of substance regarding where Jasper Wilke had
come from originally or where he was heading when he

left the Circle-S. The two investigators left with a prime suspect. But where that suspect had gotten to in the six days that had elapsed since he'd destroyed Soames's herd was the darkest of mysteries.

Two hundred yards from Soames's ranch Raider pulled up, got out a silver dollar, and, setting it on his thumb, prepared to flip it.

"Heads, west; tails, east."

"Don't be absurd. The first thing we do is ride into Wealthy and question people."

He was absolutely right, mused Raider, but he refused to acknowledge it, letting his partner ride by him and following in his dust. Mr. hard-boiled hat and funny fat pants was a lot of things sorry, he thought, but one thing he wasn't: stupid.

CHAPTER SEVEN

Poindexter's Saloon and Dance Hall, set squarely in the center of Blacktower, was a nondescript-looking barn of a place, one of a number of mail-order buildings prefabricated in the East and shipped to the early settlers of the Santa Fe Railroad hamlet. It was crowded with merrymakers, every table occupied, and Doc and Eustace were obliged to wait their turn before getting their elbows down on the bar. Each of the preceding three days of their trip north to Blacktower from Baptist Wells had been blessed by a thunderstorm, brief deluges that broke the back of the drought and dispelled the conviction that all water was warm, brackish, filled with gypsum and silt. The coming of the rain seemed to lift everyone's spirits, and the clamor filling Poindexter's put Doc in mind of a primitive tribe's after-the-rain dance, a community display of gratitude for deliverance at last from the wrath of the sun beast.

"What's your preference, gents?" asked the bartender, a flaxen-haired wraith with a mustache that looked at first glance to be longer on one side than the other. False teeth, ill-fitting and as deathly white as a washbasin, opened to deliver the question.

"Two Forty-rod," said Doc, laying a silver dollar on the bar.

They were speedily served and a large puddle of spilled beer dexterously wiped from the square foot of mahogany alloted their elbows and tumblers.

"Drink it slowly, Eustace," cautioned Doc. "Chug-a-lugging won't prove you've got hair on your chest to anybody in this crowd."

73

"I'm thirsty, Doc."

"Then get yourself a beer first."

"Don't like beer." Up went the tumbler, down came the whiskey, and down the glass, as empty as the bartender's eyes.

"Good Lord," said Doc dejectedly. "Didn't you just hear what I said?"

"What was that?"

"Never mind."

Eustace ordered a second drink. When it came, Doc pushed it to the far edge of the bar.

"Give your throat and your stomach a moment or two to recover."

Eustace shrugged good-naturedly and looked about. It wasn't difficult, standing as he did nearly six inches taller than anyone in close proximity to him.

"Folks sure are having a grand time. I think I'll get me a little girl and kick up my heels."

"Go right ahead."

Out shot Eustace's hand, seizing the drink and hurling it down. Doc sighed soundlessly and reserved comment. He had gotten to know Eustace Hillbank quite well over the past two weeks; for one thing, he knew that Eustace didn't ignore his advice out of pique or to demonstrate defiance. Eustace's problem was that he couldn't keep any suggestion, any thought in his head for longer than two seconds set back to back. Whatever advice Doc might give him, that which followed—interruption, distraction, anything—invariably drove the first intelligence cleanly out of mind.

Dancing would be good for him, reflected Doc. It would keep him out of mischief. Eustace was polite with women, warm and winning, and patently oblivious to the possibility that his homeliness might prove a barrier to social success.

"Bartender?" Doc gestured the man over. "Got a second?"

"Maybe one, mister. Me and Fred ain't exactly loafing on the job here, as you can plainly see."

"Do you happen to know a party by the name of Lester Sutherland?"

The bartender let it sink in, then shook his head.

"He's a drummer, at least he was. Specialized in yard goods. Liked to gamble, anything, but he preferred stud. Tall, about six foot two, thin, dark-haired, good-looking, mustache, always dressed to the hilt. And expensively: silk vests, tailored suits, imported shoes."

The bartender served to nearby patrons as he listened. Again he shook his head.

"Only drummer in this town these days, only one I know of is a feller from St. Louis sells farm equipment. Comes through every year about this time. Always seems to bring the rain. Makes him welcome, you bet. What'd you say your feller's name was again?"

"Lester Sutherland. Though it's possible he's using an alias."

"That a fact? On the run is he?"

A warning bell sounded silently in Doc's mind. The bartender was being much too helpful and much too negative at the same time, professing one, displaying the other. Doc glanced about. Unquestionably, this was precisely the sort of place Lester Sutherland would make his headquarters in Blacktower, unless Ellie Titus managed to put the damper on his after-work activities. The bartender continued his loquacious show of ignorance.

"Natty dresser, you say. Not too many o' the boys dress up in this town, not silk vests and tailored suits. Most don't even get into a boiled shirt, except for church on Sundays."

The music stopped suddenly; loud voices could be heard at the far corner of the crowd.

"Take that back, you meat-nosed son of a bitch!"

This summary demand was immediately followed by the unmistakable sound of fist striking bone. The crowd oohed and ahed. Doc's heart sank as intuition rose like a small snake in a corner of his mind. The crowd parted, permitting Eustace to walk out of the corner. He was towing a pert little blonde with little-girl breasts—their lower thirds covered by the top of her dress—a turned-up nose, and a well-practiced pout. Behind them on the floor, gingerly massaging his jaw, stretched a muscular-looking middle-aged man in a claw-hammer coat and string tie, his hair disheveled, his eyes rigid with shock.

"Hi, Doc, meet Florry-Mae. Florry-Mae, this is my friend."

·"Hello, Florry-Mae. Hello, Eustace. Why did you hit the man? What did he say to you? Why don't you turn right around, go back, and tell him you're sorry."

"I can't. He insulted Florry-Mae. Called her a damned floozie."

"And what did you call him?"

"Stink-breath jackass!"

"And he called you a meat-nosed son of a whatever."

"That's when I hit him. Only really because he called Florry-Mae here a floozie."

"He swung first, mister. Eustace here took it right in the brisket 'thout winking an eye." Florry-Mae beamed at him in admiration.

"I didn't hit, Doc, I hit back."

"Maybe you two ought to get yourselves a little air." Doc looked past them at the scene of the crime. "Your friend's up on his feet now, and he looks to be eager to pick up where you left off."

"Let him come." Up came Eustace's fist. "I'll give him another taste o' what for."

"Florry-Mae, be a dear and get him out of here, please?"

She nodded agreeably and marched Eustace out.

"Good thinking, friend," said the bartender to Doc. "Two punches is all Poindexter allows; any more it's classified as a brawl. Peace on earth, good will to men. House slogan."

"Mmmm." Doc finished his drink. "I didn't happen to ring any late bells on Lester Sutherland, did I?"

" 'fraid not. Sorry."

"Thanks, anyway."

Doc left, convinced without the slightest doubt that the bartender, whatever his reason might be, was lying in his mail-order teeth. Doc's unshakable faith in his instincts was immediately rewarded. Outside he caught up with Eustace and Florry-Mae.

"Guess what, Doc? Florry-Mae here knows Lester Sutherland. What do you think of that, Doc?"

"I think it's marvelous." He jerked his thumb toward Poindexter's. "You know him from there?"

She nodded. "He practically lived there."

"Lived? You mean he's moved on?"

"In a manner of speaking. He's dead."

Doc blanched. A hay wagon trundled by, tossing mud from under its near rear wheel onto his trouser leg. He paid no attention to it.

"Are you absolutely certain?"

"Well, I ain't seen the body or nothing, but that's what folks say."

Doc took her by one arm and started her up the street, the fully flounced hem of her knee-high skirt swinging easily, revealing one knee, then the other. The dyed black ostrich feather in her hair bounced up and down gaily.

"Exactly what are folks saying?"

"Well, Lester, he was playing stud one night back there at Poindexter's and he lost real heavy. He quit about eight o' clock, left, went straight to the Reverend Culpepper's house, broke in, and was robbing the reverend's strongbox when the reverend came home and surprised him. Lester shot him in the back and walked out with close to two hundred dollars. He went right back to the game, got back in, and was playing when word got out that the reverend had been robbed and murdered. They found his body facedown on the floor, a bullet in his back. Then Buford Phillips's boy Wardell put the icing on the cake. Came forward and said he'd actually seen the drummer, meaning Lester, going into Reverend Culpepper's house just before the reverend got home. Lester got wind the jig was up and left town. Lit out so fast, he didn't even stop to pack. Rode off with the clothes on his back."

"And the Reverend Culpepper's money in his pocket."

"Plus what he won with it when he got back into the game. Nearly doubled it in less than half an hour, so they say."

"They caught up with him."

She nodded. "Over someplace in the Oklahoma Panhandle, Buford Phillips and three others, all Congregationalists, regulars in Reverend Culpepper's church. They lynched Lester. Then just yesterday, guess what?"

"Let me try a wild guess. The Phillips boy let slip that he wasn't all that certain that it was Lester he saw sneaking into the minister's house."

Florry-Mae wide-eyed him. "How did you know that?"

"Wild guess."

"Poor Lester. He should have stayed put and faced the music."

"He panicked," said Doc. "I can't say I blame him. He was a stranger in town, the Phillips boy was an eyewitness, Lester did leave the game broke, then turned around and came back with two hundred dollars. Tell me something, was that the exact amount missing from the reverend's strongbox, or is everybody just putting two and two together?"

"I don't know. Whatever it was, guilty or not, Lester's dead and gone now. Snappy dresser, like you. Good dancer, too."

"When did he first come to town?"

"I can't say exactly. He was here at least a couple months."

"Was there anybody traveling with him, maybe a woman in her late twenties, beautiful natural blond hair, green eyes, superb figure. Her name's Ellie Titus, unless she's calling herself something else."

"I don't know that anybody was with him. I don't think there was."

They crossed the street and stood under the awning overhanging the door to the Blacktower Feed and Grain Store. The night air was pleasantly cool. The stars were hard and flat-looking, resembling pieces of ice. The muf-

fled sound of music drifted toward them from the saloon.
A breeze dusted a lone tumbleweed down the all-but-
deserted street.

"Hey, Doc," said Eustace. "That's helpful, isn't it?"
He nodded vigorous reassurance to Florry-Mae and squeezed
her hand.

"It is."

"Doc?"

"What?"

"What's a floozie?"

"A whore," said Florry-Mae. Swinging about, facing
Doc with her back to Eustace, she winked and grinned
impishly.

A man walked by, dragging his left leg slightly. He
wore hair chaps, studded wrist gauntlets, a leather vest too
large for him, and a five-inch-brim Stetson that all but
consumed his head. He looked ridiculous, like a boy trying
to pass himself off as a man. He was thin and very small,
no bigger than an eleven-year-old, and he squinted at them
peculiarly in passing. His face wore a troubled expression.
Eyeing him casually as he passed, Doc got the fleeting
impression that he was mad at the world and happy to
show it. He walked on without looking back, the oversized
rowels of his spurs jingling loudly. He crossed the street,
heading in the direction of Poindexter's.

"Florry-Mae," said Eustace. "Want to go to bed?"

Doc groaned silently.

"Sure," she said, bouncing up and kissing Eustace on
the cheek.

Doc groaned aloud. They started off.

"See you later, Doc," called Eustace back over his
shoulder.

Doc stood in the shadows, lighting a cheroot, listening
to the music, watching Mr. Stetson pass through the batwing doors and enter Poindexter's. Doc got out his billfold
and, by the light of the moon, examined the photograph of
Erland Titus that Uriah Swinburne had cut out of the
newspaper for him. The face in the picture was slender,
sensitive-looking, the face of one easily bruised; the nose

was aquiline, the eyes light, probably blue, thought Doc. Titus's hair was thinning; he combed the survivors straight back from his somewhat lofty forehead. Poor man, reflected Doc, refolding the picture and restoring it to his billfold. Had he found his way to Blacktower? Had he met up with Sutherland? More importantly, had he located his wayward wife? For some inexplicable reason, nothing he could immediately put his finger on, Doc got the feeling that Titus had indeed made his way to Blacktower and, moreover, was still around. If not in town, somewhere nearby.

Why, he wondered, had Ellie and Sutherland broken up? Florry-Mae didn't associate her with the drummer, couldn't make any connection between the two; evidently, they hadn't been seen together. Florry-Mae would know; Sutherland frequented Poindexter's. Perhaps Ellie wouldn't be stationed at his shoulder during the card games, but if they were still going together, she would certainly be seen with him elsewhere about town.

So many questions. Where was Erland? Where was Ellie? Where was the gang that had emptied the bank?

Doc drew deeply on his Old Virginia cheroot and, flipping the butt away, started back across the street. The music had stopped inside Poindexter's, the crowd was laughing heartily. He pushed inside. At the far end of the bar stood a cowhand with the face of an angel and shoulders the size of derby crowns separated by a full yard of sinew and bone. One arm was outstretched in front of him; suspended from the end of it, held by his shirt collar, the little man in the big clothes jiggled and jounced, dancing on air, his legs pumping, his small fists flailing away at his tormentor's face, missing it by a wide margin. Mr. Stetson, his hat hanging down his back, blued the air with curses and threats. The louder the crowd roared, the redder he became, the more violent and profane, and the more frustrated over his inability to reach the man at the other end of the arm. Finally, the cowhand set him down, spanked him lightly in the seat, and pushed him away.

"Make tracks, Billy the Kid, it's past your bedtime."

Once more the onlookers laughed uproariously. The crimson in the little man's cheeks deepened perceptibly. He backed away, his face red, his hand stealing to his guns.

"Leave 'em be," snapped the bartender, bringing a rifle up over the bar. "Just get out and don't come back."

The red-faced one continued backing toward the door. Doc sidestepped to let him pass.

"You bastards and bitches ain't seen the last o' me. I'll be back. I'll getcha, all o' you."

"Run for the hills!" bawled a man at the rear. "Dangerous Dan's come to town!"

Again laughter, raucous and cruel. Doc felt a twinge of pity for the little man. He vanished into the street, shaking his fist, hurling threats and vows of vengeance.

"What was that all about?" asked Doc, squeezing in between two burly railroad workers and catching the bartender's attention.

"He got fresh with one of the ladies. Came swaggering in here, spurs ringing like church bells. Asked Zora over there to dance, and she began giggling. She's a giggler, Zora is. He said something. She didn't like it." He shrugged. "Zora's got friends. They don't take kindly to little squirt strangers calling her down."

"You think he'll be back?"

"If he wants to put on another show he will. What's your pleasure? Forty-rod, wasn't it?"

Doc sipped for an hour, watching the faro game, watching the dancers and listening to the piano being pounded through such frontier classics as "Hog Drivers":

Hog drivers, hog drivers, hog drivers we air,
A-courtin' yer dar-ter so sweet and fair. . . .
    And "Old Joe Clark":
Well, I wish I had a nickel, I wish I had a dime,
I wish I had a purty gal to kiss and call her mine. . . .

Shortly after eleven, he decided that Eustace and Florry-Mae must have completed their tumbling by now and dropped off to sleep. Out of respect for young love, he would check into another room, one just down the hall from his and Eustace's, he decided. He started for the Hotel Blodgett. Few people were in the street; there was no sign of Mr. Stetson. What a life, thought Doc, to be five foot two in a six-foot world, with too much hat, too much mouth, and too big a chip on his skinny, sloping shoulder. By the time he'd backed out the door his complexion was well on its way to purple. Amazing he hadn't burst a blood vessel. He'd be back, all right, probably around two in the morning with a match in one hand and a can of kerosene in the other.

The desk clerk dozed on his forearm, his pate shining pink in the feeble light of his lamp. Doc shook him, woke him, and got another room. Ascending to the third floor, wandering down the dimly lit, bare-boarded hallway, he was about to thrust his key into the lock when he hesitated and went stealthily back up the hall to his old room. Planting his ear against the door, he listened. The iron bed sounded as if it were on the verge of collapsing in a twisted heap; over its demise rose a sound resembling a slush pump in violent action; groaning, grunting, and squealing assailed Doc's ear. He sighed, went to his room, prepared for bed, and, blowing out the lamp, went to sleep.

Eustace, meanwhile, had mounted Florry-Mae for the fifth time, thrusting his enormous rod base deep into her ample and accommodating quim, rolling the two of them over so conjoined, grabbing her buttocks and holding on for dear life as she cunt-danced wildly, grinding and bouncing, slamming down, jerking up, swinging, swaying, pummeling his meat relentlessly, filling his helpless balls to a temper comparable to that of the round cast-steel heads of two two-pound Y. & P. Brand Machinists' Ball Peen Hammers.

Fifteen minutes of pure barbaric frenzy later, Eustace unloaded, Florry-Mae squealing with joy, coming for the fourth time simultaneously with his ejaculation and grinding her apparatus to rest, tumbling off him in exhaustion.

"Florry-Mae?" he murmured.

"Yeah?"

"Will you marry me?"

"Sure, when?"

"In the morning." Pause. "Florry-Mae?"

"Yeah?"

"I'm getting hard again."

"Good. Good, good, good, good, good!"

Doc was awakened by a loud pounding on his door. Dragging himself out of bed and into his trousers, he stumbled toward it.

"Who is it?"

"Me, Eustace."

"What time is it?"

"Late, getting on to five o'clock. Sun's coming up. 'sgoing to be a beautiful day. Open the door."

"Eustace . . . Oh, what the hell."

He swung wide the door. There stood Eustace, fully dressed, Florry-Mae by his side. She was powdered and rouged and smiling, every hair in place under her feather, but her heavily mascaraed eyes looked as if they'd been splattered with ketchup.

"Good morning, Florry-Mae," said Doc solicitously.

"Morning, Doc."

Eustace beamed. "Doc, we got big news."

"Big enough to wake me up at five in the morning?"

"Me and Florry-Mae are getting hitched. I proposed, and she accepted. I'm going to buy her a ring and everything."

Doc sighed and leaned against the jamb for support. "Eustace . . ."

"Doc, I'm quitting being an operative. I'm going to settle down right here in Blacktower."

It was as far as he got; shooting his arm out, Doc snatched a handful of his shirt and hauled him bodily into the room.

"Florry-Mae, if you'll excuse us, he'll be with you in a couple minutes."

"I'll be waiting down in the lobby, sweety lumps."

"Excuse me." Doc shut the door in her smile.

"Listen to me, sweety lumps."

"Don't try to talk me out of it, Doc. We're in love, and we're getting hitched."

"Blessings on you both. By all means do so, if that's what you want. Only not today. Not tomorrow, either. It happens we're smack in the middle of a case. You can't just drop it like a hot potato; it's not right, Eustace. It's not professional. It would be a rotten thing to do to your Uncle Bill, not to mention Mr. Pinkerton. The two of them have high hopes for you. Great faith in your potential. Eustace, you're not the sort who lets people down, are you? You're no quitter. That's what you'll be if you back out now. You made a commitment."

"When will we be finished?"

"Soon. We're hot on the trail. Maybe today we'll turn up Mr. Titus. Maybe Mrs. Titus, too. Once we do, we'll be in the homestretch. I'll be honest, Eustace, I need you. Mightily. I can't handle this thing alone."

Eustace smiled proudly, pulling himself up, inflating his chest.

"We're a team, son. You can't go breaking up a team. Not in the middle of a case. All I'm asking is that you hold off until we wind things up. Florry-Mae'll wait. She'll understand. The very day we're done, you can marry her. I'll be your best man if you want me."

"I hope to tell we do." The light in his eyes faded. "You're right. Uncle Bill wouldn't like me quitting on you. I'll go down and tell Florry-Mae. It'll be okay. She'll understand."

"I'm sure she will. She's a gem, that girl. And she's important to the case. Didn't she give us all that information about Sutherland?"

"Who?"

"The drummer."

"You bet she did. I'll go down and talk to her. You come down and we'll all have breakfast together."

He left. Closing the door, Doc leaned against it and took a deep, shuddering breath. Great day in the morning, he thought, sending sweety lumps back to Uncle Bill and Allan Pinkerton married to a dance-hall floozie, even one as cute and sweet as Florry-Mae, would be like sending him home with two bullets in him.

"Either way, you come up the loser," he said, addressing the man in the cracked and yellowed mirror above the washstand.

He sighed. "Young love, young love, young love."

Moving back to the bed, he toppled over onto it facedown.

CHAPTER EIGHT

Extricating Eustace from the arms of the love of his life, Doc walked him down to the livery stable and the two of them fed Judith a breakfast of carefully selected oats and cool, fresh water. They spent most of the morning questioning townspeople, describing Ellie Titus in detail, but no one appeared to recognize her. Around noontime, they returned to the stable and rented horses—a big blood bay for Eustace that the young giant speedily dwarfed as he settled his bulk in his saddle.

"Where we heading, Doc?"

"I want to ride a spiral around town, a widening circle: I want to see what's out there—mines, deserted cabins, any place people can hide out." He unfolded a map. "We're on the western edge of the Llano Estacado, what they call in Texas the Staked Plains. Not many trees, except cotton-wood and willows along the streams. Cactus, yucca. Fairly arid, barren." He pointed south, indicating a huge mesa cloaked in velvet shadows. "That flattop is where the town gets its name. You'll see mesas all over the region."

"You think Mr. Titus is out there somewhere?"

"I've a hunch he's looking for Mrs. Titus. Sutherland's settling here is proof of that—enough for me."

"What if she didn't come this far with him?" Doc's face fell. It was a possibility that hadn't occurred to him. "Nobody we've talked to seems to recognize her," added Eustace.

"True."

"Could be she's never come near here."

"She left Baptist Wells with him." Which proved nothing after the fact, which realization, he decided, made his tone suddenly sound so lame.

"They could have had a spat on the way and parted company."

"Possibly." Doc shifted his weight uneasily in his saddle. Eustace was no doubt absolutely right. It certainly explained their failure to find her in spite of the drummer's arrival.

"Maybe we're going about this thing all wrong," he said quietly. "Maybe I am . . ."

He looked off up the street as he spoke. He paused and stared. He squeezed his eyes shut, opened them again, gasped, and marveled. Were they deceiving him? He got out his billfold, produced Titus's picture, studied it, and looked up again at the man riding toward them on a coyote dun mare with white stockings. He had removed his slouch hat and was fanning himself with it. Doc looked down at the picture again, comparing, then he handed it to Eustace.

"It's him, Titus!"

"That fellow's got a beard."

"I don't care, it's him. Look at that nose, that high forehead, the way he combs his hair. That's Erland Titus."

"Let's get him!"

"Hold it. Sit tight, let's see where he's heading."

The bearded man, without the slightest doubt Erland Titus in Doc's mind, reined up at a public hitch rack, tied up his mount, and entered the Waffle House Restaurant.

"Let's get us some lunch, Doc."

Again Doc stayed him, grabbing his forearm. Then he changed his mind.

"Okay, if you're hungry, get yourself a quick bite. Any place but there. I'll stick here and keep an eye on the door."

Eustace dismounted and handed his reins to him.

"Make it fast," added Doc.

Eustace hurried off in the opposite direction. Doc sat his horse, waiting with growing impatience; but at the same time, a warm feeling was rising in his chest. What luck! Blind luck. It came so rarely in this line especially, so few god-given breaks to make up for the grief and misfortune that dogged him, dogged every operative; the delays, false leads, mix-ups, mischances, calamities, and downright disasters. He had hesitated to show Titus's picture to anybody around town for fear that if he were in town someone who recognized him from the picture might warn him. He and Eustace were running the same risk with Mrs. Titus, to be sure, but at least she wasn't the prime suspect.

This was a break; what a break! Go get him? Never, Eustace. That would be the last thing they'd do; the first is to shadow him, dog him wherever he goes. He might just lead them to the money.

Was the old axiom true, he wondered. Did good luck like bad always come in threes? Spot Erland, follow him to the money, locate the gang, possibly even Ellie, although that would make it four. At that, they didn't need her, not now, now that they'd found Erland.

"Eustace," murmured Doc to himself, "you may become a bridegroom quicker than you know. Great God, what am I saying!"

The sun baked Blacktower. A mischievous and searing breeze chased dust and tumbleweeds up and down the main street. All was quiet in Poindexter's, the building at rest—no doubt recovering from the hubbub and clangor it had suffered through the night before, Doc reflected. Mr. Stetson had not returned with his grudge and a torch. Ignoring the heat, two dogs snarled and bit their way through a brief to-do in front of the Waffle House, bringing a waitress out wielding a broom. The sun seemed to grow fiercer; the pale blue sky showed no clouds, no sign of a more than welcome afternoon rainstorm.

Eustace returned, his smile full of roast beef, a home-baked bread and beef sandwich in a paper sack for Doc. Moments later Erland Titus emerged from the restaurant, remounted his horse, swung about, and rode off the way he came.

Doc gave him a two-minute head start, then they followed.

CHAPTER NINE

"Who's that?" inquired Raider. "Your mother?"

Algernon drew himself up haughtily, impaling him with a withering glare. "That, Raider, as you so coarsely put it, is Victoria, the Queen of England."

Raider studied the round-faced, imperious-looking, middle-aged woman, noticing the delicate tiara all but concealed by her hair.

"She's got kind of a skimpy crown, hasn't she?"

"It's a tiara."

"Oh."

Algernon had unpacked his oversized saddlebags, and placed the framed portrait of Victoria on top of the bureau, angling it to catch the sunlight pouring through the window. He stood briefly transfixed in admiration of the first and grandest lady of the British Empire.

"Careful what you say, old boy, you are looking at the greatest woman who has ever lived," said Algernon solemnly, "the epitome of royalty, one which involves none of the mischiefs of caprice or ostentation, a woman who serves not only her people, but the entire world as an example alike of motherly sympathy and of queenly dignity."

"That's real nice."

Algernon glowered. " 'Real nice.' "

It was the first time in their association that the two had been obliged to share a room, the first time since Topeka that they would not be sleeping in their bedrolls under the stars. They had earlier deserted Texas County, heading west into Cimarron, passing through Willowbar and reach-

ing Boise City, the county seat. On the way, they had run
into a dust storm. Riding along, Raider had caught sight of
an immense bank of reddish-brown and blue-black clouds
to the north and west. They came boiling, rolling, and
tumbling silently toward them, like seething smoke pouring out of a burning building. At the sight a panicky
feeling took possession of him. For an instant, he imagined it was the end of the world. A black blanket engulfed
them; blinding, choking dust settled over them. They covered their horse's muzzles and their own faces, kneeling
with their backs to the onslaught.

The intense darkness and whirling, flesh-grating fury
went on for less than an hour; then the sun gradually
emerged, first in a hazy, muddy color, then finally, around
four o'clock, burning through the lingering dust in blood-
red rays.

The Mistletoe Hotel in Boise City appeared on the verge
of collapse, but it offered the only public accommodations
in town. To the chagrin of both operatives, only one room
was available. Only one bed. The two had not even finished unpacking before it became clear to Raider that their
minor differences of opinion, the disparity in their back-
grounds, upbringings, educations, and a host of other fac-
tors promised to be egregiously intensified by the present
arrangement. Fortunately, the tension found some relief in
a welcome turn of events in the case. Before stabling their
horses and checking into the hotel, Algernon had insisted
on wiring Wagner in Chicago to report their findings to
date. A long message in code came back to them in
response. Now Raider sat on the edge of the discourag-
ingly narrow wooden bed, crunching the tick mattress with
his weight, patiently decoding Wagner's reply. Algernon
paced up and down the little room, frowning at the depress-
ing surroundings, the cheap, battered furnishings, the crack
in the washbasin, the telltale odor of stale vomit, and the
curtainless and shadeless window, missing one pane. Now
and then he would cast a worshipful eye at the portrait of
his queen, following it with a jaundiced eye at Raider.

Raider whistled softly.

"What?" asked Algernon.

"Our little friend with the bad eyes and the bum knee looks to be changing lines."

"What are you talking about?"

Raider tapped the telegram unfolded on his lap. "This from Chicago is more or less a recap of a news item that ran in most of the papers in New Mexico a couple days back. It has to do with a place called Blacktower, a saloon–dance hall called Poindexter's. Somebody spiked one or maybe more whiskey barrels with you know what." He nodded sagely. "Seventeen dead."

"You think it was our man?"

"Who else could it be? He hasn't poisoned another herd in more than ten days. Common sense says he must have pulled out of the Panhandle. I mean, you don't do what he did and hang around to hear the moaning and groaning. He had to go someplace." He tapped the paper. "This says over the border to this Blacktower."

"You could be right," said Algernon, his tone unmistakably begrudging. "We've established that the bounder's motive is vengeance. It's quite possible he wished to get even for some real or imagined slight."

"Which he plainly got at this joint, Poindexter's. Maybe the barkeep looked at him cross-eyed. It does fit, Algernon. As far as he's concerned, he's gotten even in spades with Hansen, Soames, and the other cattle ranchers who fired him. He's a roaring success. He sure thinks so. So successful, anybody crosses him now is signing his or her own death warrant."

"Seventeen people dead, you say?"

"Maybe even more. That's likely only the first tally, though you can bet the law's closed up the place faster'n you can shake a stick."

Algernon was nodding, ruminating, chewing over the news, and—from his expression, mused Raider—entirely agreeing with his assessment of it.

"Surprise, surprise," mused Raider aloud.

"Isn't it . . ."

"I don't mean Jasper Wilke or whatever name he's

using these days, I mean us seeing eye to eye on something. To be honest, I never thought I'd live to see the day.''

"Come now, old chap, even you have to be correct in your assessment of a situation once in the proverbial blue moon. Nobody can be wrong one hundred percent of the time.''

"Thanks, you got a good heart." He glanced about the room. "I won't be sorry to say good-bye to this shithole bright and early tomorrow. You hungry?"

"Utterly famished."

Raider exhaled sharply. "Can't you just say yes or no?"

"Shall we freshen up and hie ourself to the nearest halfway decent-looking restaurant?"

They sat in a gloomy little dining room over steak and potatoes, Algernon complaining as usual over the limitations of the menu. The place was filled with diners, too many tables were crammed into the little room, and the two waitresses sharing the obligations of fetching, carrying, listening to complaints, and writing up tabs were harried and hurried to distraction. When the coffee arrived, late and cooled by the delay, Algernon's patience—held in check by Raider's soothing admonitions—burst its seams.

"See here, my girl," he blustered. "This filthy muck is ice cold. Bring me a fresh cup, top of the pot and hot. Immediately!"

"Algernon," began Raider, his eyes darting back and forth at the diners nearby, all of whom had suddenly stopped eating and were looking on with mouths agape.

"Mister," began the waitress, a frowzy, thin-as-a-bird's-leg, middle-aged woman with hair like brown straw and grease spots all over her blouse and apron.

"No excuses, no apologies, please. Simply do as I tell you!"

The waitress threw up her hands in surrender and scurried away. A short, homely man with a beard badly in need of trimming and brushing cleared his throat and leaned over to Algernon.

"Brother, you oughtn'ta talk to Elvirey thattaway. Cain't

you see she's got her hands full? Poor thing's doin' the bes' she can.''

"Her 'bes' is none to good, 'brother,' and would you kindly tend to your own affairs?''

"Now jes' a damn minute!''

"Algernon,'' began Raider.

Algernon snarled at the intruder and dismissed him with a melodramatic wave of his hand. The man lurched to his feet, whipped his napkin from his collar, and slammed it on the table. His three companions also stood up. One of them, noted Raider, was bigger and broader than Algernon; another was equal to him in bulk. All four were wearing guns.

Algernon stared at one, then the others in turn, contempt deepening his scowl.

"Ahhhh, what have we here, the Boise City Committee for Municipal Improvement? Take your seats, chaps, everyone's staring at you. You're making a public spectacle of yourselves.''

"Algernon . . .''

The short man glanced at Raider. "What'd he say?''

"Not a thing, mister. Nothing to get riled about. Let's just all keep calm.''

"Hey, Mac,'' yelled a voice, "look over to the corner. Elvira's crying her eyes out, poor soul.''

In the far corner stood Elvira—her apron off, crumpled in a ball—massaging away tears.

"See what you did!'' bawled the short man. "You got her all upset, bawlin' her out like you done. On your feet, dude. You and me's goin' outside an' have at it!''

"You an' me is goin' nowhere, little man. Certainly not before she serves me my coffee.'' He turned in his chair, raising his hand, snapping his fingers. "You there, Elvira. I want my coffee, and I want it now!''

"Jesus Christ,'' murmured Raider, lowering his head and making a conscious if wasted effort to crawl under the edge of his plate.

Elvira had heard. Lowering her apron slowly, she stared for a split second, then broke out in a new flood of tears, caterwauling loudly. By now the entire dining room was enjoying the show. The short man swore vilely, grabbed Algernon by the shoulder, was shaken off, hauled off, and swung. Algernon ducked. Raider caught the punch in the side of the head, ringing bells and briefly spinning the room. Algernon flattened the man with one punch. His three companions roared and leaped to the attack. At once, as if a switch had been thrown, bedlam reigned. Fights broke out at every other table. Chairs were swung and smashed, tables overturned, cups and plates shattered against the walls. Ducking, grabbing Algernon by the sleeve, Raider pulled him toward the kitchen door a few steps from their table. Through the kitchen they ran, past the astonished cook, his helper, and the other waitress, and out the back door. Algernon started left. Again Raider grabbed him, pulling him right.

"This way to the Mistletoe, stupid!"

They ran and ran and reached the hotel in short order, racing up the stairs to their room. Algernon dropped onto the bed, gasping for breath.

"What are we running for? And see here, you called me stupid!"

"Stupid, dumb, thick-headed . . ." Raider's hand stole to the aching side of his head. "I ought to bust you in little pieces, you asshole! You and your big mouth!"

"See here, old boy, all I wanted was a fresh cup of coffee."

"Oh, Jesus! Don't just sit there, damn it, get busy and get packing. We got to move. That bunch is out looking for us. We got to get outta town before they run us out—tar, feathers, the whole kaboodle!"

Eight minutes later they were on their way, riding west into the blazing, lowering sun, kicking up a cloud of dust so thick it effectively obscured Boise City behind them. They rode at a gallop for two miles before Raider reined up. Algernon pulled up alongside.

"We're in the clear, old boy, there's no one coming." He glanced left and right and straight ahead. The road curved abruptly about a hundred yards around a huge, sprawling outcropping studded with cactus. Sagebrush abounded, its green paled perceptibly by the merciless sun.

A shot rang out, splitting the silence, lead plowing through the top of Raider's hat, dropping his head into his neck like a turtle's. Hurling himself clear, at the same time slipping the Winchester from its boot, he rolled down into a gully.

"Get down here, you asshole, before you get blown down!"

A rain of shots punctuated this advice. Algernon hit on all fours, rolling over, coming up beside him, losing his derby and reacting irritably. Raider sneaked a peek at the outcropping. Four more shots sounded, tiny puffs of smoke betraying the positions of the bushwhackers. Sand kicked high six inches in front of Algernon's head, lying facedown. The other three shots thudded close, bracketing them.

"Jesus Christ," groaned Raider. "We're about as safe here as in a damn fish bowl!"

Algernon shot a quick glance to their left.

"How about those boulders?"

Raider measured the distance to the infinitely better protection of four huge boulders in a tight grouping. Less than thirty feet separated the two from them. Raider dug out his six-gun and thrust the Winchester at Algernon.

"I'm trying it. Cover me. Pour it on. When I count three . . ."

"Very well, Raider."

"What?"

"Who do you suppose that is up there?"

"Who in hell do you think?"

Algernon gasped. "It's ridiculous. Human beings don't shoot one another over a trifling difference of opinion."

"Who says the bastards are human? Big-mouth. I'm counting." He took a deep breath; Algernon scrunched lower and took aim. Again firing came from the outcropping. "One, two, . . . three," said Raider huskily, springing to his feet and fast-crabbing to the boulders, his six-gun blazing. Behind him, Algernon emptied the Winchester rapid-fire.

"Raider, oh, Raider. I'm out of cartridges!"

Raider glared. "A little louder, maybe one of 'em doesn't hear so good."

Reaching into his breast pocket, he got out a box of .30-.30s and tossed them back. Then he began to reload his own gun.

Lead flew heavily back and forth for the next few minutes. Algernon didn't dare to chance following Raider's lead for fear of giving the ambushers an even better target than he was already providing. Raider reloaded a fourth time and called to him.

"Hey!" He lowered his voice. "I think one or two are right behind that sharp rock, the one sticking up at an angle. See there? Keep a close eye on it. Anything you see move, gun it down."

"Done."

He was as good as his word. Something moved; he fired. A loud scream followed the echo, and a man tumbled out from behind the rock, clutching his head. A second man foolishly started up, as if moving to help him. He caught a shot squarely in the face, turning it into a beautiful crimson flower before his body hit.

"Good shooting," called out Raider. "Great. I wish we had the other rifle, though. Why in hell you can't boot it up front where it's handy instead of in your damn saddlebags is beyond me."

"Let's not have tears over spilt milk, old chap."

"We could end up spilling more than milk."

A single shot rang out. Algernon grunted, his body jerking as if an electric shock had passed through it. He buried his face in the sand.

"Hey!" called Raider.

"My shoulder."

"Bad?"

"It missed the bone, I think."

"Belly a little to your right and back, can you? It looks to be a little deeper there, give yourself better protection. Toss me back the rifle." Algernon did so. "And the cartridges. Make sure the top's tight. We don't want to scatter 'em.''

Algernon tossed the half-filled box of cartridges; it hit, the top flew open, the contents scattering.

"Oh, for Chrissakes!"

Raider recovered a handful of cartridges and reloaded the Winchester. The two surviving bushwhackers had stopped firing for the moment. One called out.

"Hey, you two. It's a Mex standoff. Want to call it quits?"

Raider recognized the little man's high-pitched voice.

"Makes sense to me," said Raider.

Algernon gasped. "You're not about to take his word, are you? It's a trick!"

"Want to?" the voice repeated. "I'll count three, we'll both stand up, show ourselves, toss down our weapons, and raise our hands. You do the same."

"Raider!" Algernon threw a fearful glance at him.

"Go ahead!" called Raider.

"No!" Algernon glared at him. "You're playing right into their hands. I tell you it's a trick!"

"It's okay," said Raider calmly. "Get out your popgun and do like I tell you."

"But . . ."

"No damn buts!"

Up in the rocks the biggest of the four men had shown himself, tossing his pistol clattering down. The little man appeared, disposing of his rifle and lifting his hands.

Raider stood up, tossing aside the Winchester, slowly lifting his hands.

"Get up, Algernon," he muttered out of the corner of his mouth.

"See here!"

"Do it!"

Algernon rose to his feet, reluctantly tossing away his Mauser. Before it hit the ground the little man's right hand was down and twisting behind him, jerking a gun from his belt. A shot rang out. He stiffened, grunted, and pitched

forward. Algernon, his eyes fixed on him, turned slowly to
his left. Raider stood with his smoking six-gun in hand.

"Come on down, friend," he called. "Or you'll be
number four."

Algernon stared in mingled awe and admiration. "You
knew he was concealing a gun?"

"Lucky guess," said Raider drily. "I knew one thing."

"What?"

"I was."

The lone survivor approached them, his hands upraised,
his eyes darting about nervously.

"What you going to do?"

"Get down on your knees," said Raider coldly. "My
friend here is going to tie your hands behind your back,
blindfold you, and I'm going to put you outta your misery."

"Raider!" gasped Algernon.

The man swallowed a stone, his eyes saucering. "You
wouldn't!"

"I'd like to, you bastard. Where in hell you four get off
trying to dry-gulch us? How'd you know we were heading
west?"

"He said so whilst you was eating."

"Okay, drop your belt, take off your John B., kick off
your boots, and back away twenty feet."

The man nodded and speedily did so.

"Now start walking," said Raider, as Algernon col-
lected everything.

Again the man swallowed and started off, heading for
town. He stopped and turned.

"It's better'n two mile. It's hotter'n hell."

"It's going to get a lot hotter." Raider fired twice,
kicking sand up two inches from his heels. He danced
briefly and fled. Raider threw a third shot after him,
hurrying his step.

"Drop his hat and boots in the gully and kick sand over
'em. Then get the shells outta his belt and collect the rest
that scattered when you tossed the box to me. I'm going
up into the rocks and pick up their iron and ammo. When
we get done, we'll fetch the horses." He gestured. Their

two mounts were grazing contentedly in the distance. "Let's have a look at your wound."

Through the tear in Algernon's sleeve a crimson streak the size of Raider's index finger curved around the top of the Englishman's shoulder like a slender epaulet that had slipped from position.

"Just a crease, but you ought to wash it out. Got anything in those catch-all saddlebags o' yours to stanch the bleeding?"

"Witherspoon's Salve."

Raider grunted. "Cobwebs are better'n any salve. But it's your crease." He paused, eyeing him archly. "Tell me something, did you learn anything new today?"

"I admit I should have maintained my composure at dinner."

"I'll say. Mister, I can put up with your pie-plate saddle, your flasharity, your wanting to carry everything with you but the kitchen sink, your popgun, your know-it-all ways, Queen Victoria's picture staring me in the face every morning I wake up, your afternoon tea every time four o'clock comes around, wherever we are, whatever we're doing, but this business of putting everybody you talk to down in a hole, looking down your nose at them and deliberately ruffling their feathers has got to go." His tone softened, becoming almost pleading. "Algernon, man to man, I got to tell you. You know you talk different than us."

"I speak the King's English!" he snapped haughtily.

"And we don't. I'm not saying the way you pernounce your words is better than we do or vice versa, but mister, when you open your mouth it does come out different. Folks aren't used to it. They hear you and their right hand all but starts for their holster. They're suspicious—that's the general reaction to foreigners. Which is what you are out here, a foreigner. I'm not blaming you, I'm not condemning you, I'm simply saying you're different looking, sounding, acting, and right off the bat, folks get their guards up. You got to be patient with 'em, you got to give a little. Bend. Don't snap at 'em and dress 'em down."

"I'm sorry, Raider. I believe I understand what you're trying to say, but I cannot, I will not tolerate blind stupidity or the blathering of raging ignoramuses."

"You'd best learn to, and fast. Before you wind up with lead in your breakfast. Hell, you don't ruffle *some* people, even *most* people, you do it to everybody!"

"I do it to those who deserve it."

"But who in hell are you to judge? I wouldn't give two hoots who you do it to, only I'm here with you, we're working together. When you get somebody riled up at you, they get just as riled at me, and I haven't even opened my mouth." His hand went to the side of his head. The aching soreness from the punch had all but disappeared, but recollection of the incident threatened to restore it in mind if not in fact. "From here on in, please watch what you say and to who, will you? For my sake?"

"I'll get the horses. You collect their weapons. There's a good chap."

Raider sighed, started to add something further, thought better of it, and walked off. Far down the road behind him the survivor of the shoot-out continued plodding toward town.

CHAPTER TEN

Marshal Virgil Huggens of Blacktower, Curry County, New Mexico, had one working eye; the other was concealed behind a black patch. His good eye was actually none too good, decided Raider; it narrowed, squinted, and took its time focusing on him and Algernon as they plumped down tiredly into round-back chairs opposite the lawman in his office. Reposing on his desk at his elbow were twin ivory-handled Peacemakers in brand-new hand-tooled holsters suspended from twin drop loops attached to an elaborate buscadero. Alongside the desk stood a brand-new oak-stave whiskey barrel, its contents clearly stenciled top and side over the legend: Castleberry & Sons, Pittsburgh, Penna. Turning in his chair, Huggens lay the flat of his hand on the barrel.

"This is the killer, right here. Twenty-one dead, nearly twice that number sick as dogs."

Algernon got to his feet and examined the barrel. "The bung is still in place."

"That it is," said the marshal.

"Put back," said Raider. "Let me ask you this, Marshal. When the bartenders fixed on this particular barrel as the culprit, didn't they notice anything suspicious, like marks around the bunghole, marks they knew they didn't put there?"

Huggens shook his head and gestured Raider to join him. The three of them stood around the barrel.

"Whoever put the arsenic in didn't remove the bung to do it. Minot and Fred, the two bartenders over at Poindexter's, swear that when they brought this in from the

101

shed the bung hadn't been tampered with. I mean not a finger laid on it since it was delivered from the distillery. I believe 'em, Raider.''

"That's crazy! How in red hell could the poisoner put the arsenic in if he didn't pull the bung? I sure don't see any holes, do you?"

"Nope," said Huggens, a mischievous smile playing about his liver-colored lips. His one eye twinkled.

Algernon was crouching. He had gotten out a magnifying glass and was examining the upper hoop.

"I see how it was done. Look here, Raider. See the tiny scratch marks around the brads? They've been removed and put back. Neat job, I must say, but that's what was done. They've obviously been tampered with.''

"So?" Understanding dawned, slowly flooding Raider's face. "The hole's behind the hoop.''

"That's right," said Huggens.

He got a pair of pliers out of his desk drawer and, one after another, pulled the eight brads holding the hoop in place. Then he eased it upward, revealing two quarter-inch holes side by side.

"Whoever did it drained the level down to just below these holes," he said, "added the arsenic, then put back the hoop slick as new.''

"How'd you figure that out?" Raider asked Algernon.

"Pure logic, old chap. It had to be put in somewhere. Above the level of the contents, to be sure.''

"Good thinking," said Raider, all but forcing the words out. "Marshal, didn't the two bartenders think something was fishy when they opened the barrel and saw the level was down?"

Huggens shrugged. "This stuff isn't exactly sipping whiskey. For the price Poindexter pays for rotgut they don't worry too much if the barrel opens up a little short. Though Minot did mention it in passing. That's what got me to thinking about the point of entry maybe being hidden behind the hoop. So I took it off too.''

"But why put it back on?" asked Algernon in a superior tone.

"I figured if and when we caught whoever did it and put him on trial this'd be prime evidence. Exhibit A. Whoever's prosecuting could demonstrate to the judge how it was done. You got to think ahead in this business. You two should know that."

"Amen," said Raider. "Any suspects?"

Huggens's face darkened. "Not a damned one. Well one, but I'll be damned if we can locate him. Stranger in town, little fellow with a big mouth. He started a ruckus over to Poindexter's and was thrown out. He threatened everybody within earshot."

"Drunk?" asked Raider.

"Sober as the parson. That's why Minot and Fred seemed to think he might have done this. They both say he was angrier than a hornet. We've combed the area, but there's no sign of him. He's no doubt long gone, I'm afraid."

"Like my partner here told you, Marshal, we've been chasing after somebody over in the Oklahoma Panhandle who's been poisoning whole herds. We got information from headquarters in Chicago by wire. The brain trust seems to think the son of a bitch we're after did this. It does make sense."

Huggens nodded. "It does. More crazies running around than you can shake a stick at. This one's got to be stopped. I'll welcome all the help I can get." Huggens shook his head, his expression solemn. "He's won every time out so far. It's got to be going to his head."

"You said you've searched the area," interposed Algernon.

"In a circle about five miles out. We practically looked under rocks, but it was hopeless. You got to figure, if either of you did this, would *you* stick around? I sure as hell wouldn't."

"Good point," said Raider.

They said good-bye, parting company promising Huggens they would keep him abreast of the case, fill him in on anything of significance that they uncovered.

"Providing we find anything," said Raider sourly, as

they remounted their horses outside. "Which doesn't seem likely."

"I think we should get a description of the suspect from the barmen. Something a trifle more detailed than the fact that he's smallish."

"A runt in britches too big and mad at the world because of it. On account he's got to tilt his head back to look folks in the eye. I've seen the sort."

Poindexter's was closed: "Until further notice." Raider and Algernon located Minot Hornsby, the bartender, in the Waffle House, piling waffles limp with syrup into his skinny frame. He gave them an accurate description of the suspect. It tallied perfectly with Soames's description of Jasper Wilke. Raider was jubilant when they got back outside.

"Calm yourself, old fellow," cautioned Algernon. "He may be the same man, and we may know what he looks like, but finding the bounder promises to be like searching for the proverbial needle."

"I got a hunch he's still around these parts."

"You hope he is. Unfortunately, common sense dictates that there's no reason on earth why he should be. You don't for a moment imagine he's coming back here to town, do you?"

"Do I look stupid?"

Algernon eyed him jaundicedly. Raider curled his right hand into a fist. Algernon said nothing. Then he cleared his throat.

"Where shall we start?"

Clouds were massing overhead, their bellies bruised and ominous looking. The air was very still. Thunder rumbled in the distance to the north.

"Let's take a minute and figure. He sure as hell didn't head back toward No-Man's-Land. What's the next town west of here, I wonder?" Raider scratched his head. "That's no good."

"What? Come, come, be specific."

"Directly west follows the railroad. Across the Pecos River and into the Magdalenas and the Manzanos."

"It's quite possible that is precisely what he did. Bought a railway ticket and made off to heaven-knows-where."

"You're being real helpful today, Mr. Sunshine."

"I'm being realistic. He has a week's leg on us. We can safely assume he hasn't headed back the way we came, but that still leaves the rest of the compass."

"I say we get on to the next town and ask questions."

"Which 'next town'?"

"How in hell do I know? I don't know this neck o' the woods. Whatever the next town southwest is, away from the railroad, damn it!"

"Does it have a name?"

"Does your asshole? What have you suddenly got your back up for? We'll know when we get there. Let's quit palavering and get going!"

"Palavering? Delicious!"

Whipping out his little book and pencil, he wrote down the word. Raider glowered and moved off.

CHAPTER ELEVEN

A peregrine falcon floated above them on blackish-blue wings, its white belly faintly visible, its eye impaling its prey below.

"We been following him for days, Doc. All he does is sit and scratch away at his map, figuring, measuring, rolling it back up, and riding on. I'm getting saddle sore."

"So am I, Eustace. So is he."

"What's he up to, do you think?" Eustace shaded his eyes with one hand, looking at the dot on the horizon, the seated figure of Erland Titus, his horse grazing behind him.

"Isn't it obvious?" Doc lowered the binoculars and bellied closer to Eustace, handing them to him. "He's got a pencil compass and a protractor and he's sectioning off the area like slices in a pie. Every day he rides out and searches one. He's obviously been at it for weeks."

"Looking for his missus."

"So it appears."

"How come we're waiting till he finds her, if ever? I mean, he's the one we want. Why don't we cut out all this shilly-shallying, grab him, and fetch him back to Baptist Wells? You take him back . . ."

"And what are you going to do?"

Eustace beamed. "Marry Florry-Mae and settle down here."

"Eustace, Florry-Mae's being very patient. Why can't you be? Yes, we could grab him, but what about the bank, the money? Hasn't it occurred to you that the light of his life and the money may very well be holed up somewhere together?''

''But he's the one we're supposed to bring back. You said he was in on the robbery.''

''I know what I said, but I could be wrong. It has happened in the past. He could be as innocent as you are. At the moment I'm beginning to lean toward his ex. It wouldn't surprise me if Erland feels the same way, and that if he finds her, he'll find what's left of his bank.''

''She didn't have anything to do with the robbery. She was long gone with the drummer before that bunch hit town. Isn't that so?''

''It is, but she broke up with Sutherland soon after they reached Blacktower. Possibly even before. She doesn't seem the sort to go it alone for long. Pretty women rarely are. My guess is she hooked up with somebody else— whoever engineered the robbery. They picked the bank clean and didn't have to break in. They had a key, Eustace, remember? Who do you suppose gave it to them?''

The falcon, striking thirty feet from them, snatched hold of a sidewinder and flew away with it wriggling in its beak.

''Head down,'' snapped Doc. ''He's looking this way.''

Titus had turned to watch the bird, then he returned his attention to his map, rolling it up, mounting his horse, and heading out to the northwest.

''Give him a couple minutes,'' said Doc, laying a hand on Eustace's forearm as he was preparing to rise. ''This is fairly flat country. On a clear day like this he can see for miles.''

''He's heading for the foothills.''

''That's good for us. We may be able to get closer. Let me have the glasses.''

They stayed two hundred yards behind Titus. Eustace rarely had anything of value to contribute to strategy, Doc mused, as he rode along ahead of him, but at times he filled the role, albeit unconsciously, of devil's advocate. He wanted to grab Titus. Heretofore Doc had felt that they would be better off following him on the odd chance that he just might stumble upon his wife—and with her the gang. In effect, Titus was doing their searching for them; but following him did not lessen their labor. So why not join forces with him?

"Only on our terms."

"You say something, Doc?"

"Come up here alongside, Eustace. Keep your voice down. The breeze is blowing his way. I've changed my mind, I think we ought to do as you suggested, grab him."

"But you said . . ."

"Never mind. Would you please just hear me out? We grab him and pretend we're going to take him back to Baptist Wells to stand trial. He'll swear up and down he had no part in the robbery. The trouble is, that may turn out as far as he'll go."

"I don't get you, Doc."

"Don't you understand? He probably won't want to incriminate his wife, even though I'd bet my life she's in this thing up to her neck."

"You're just guessing."

"An educated guess, Eustace. You keep forgetting—the gang used a key to get into the bank."

"Maybe Mrs. Paltz lent 'em hers."

"I don't think so," said Doc patiently. "Okay, when we grab him, I'll ask the questions. Don't you say anything: about Sutherland, the money, his wife, anything. Let me handle it, promise me you will. He doesn't know what we know, even what we surmise. Let's just see if we can get him to open up. He may say something helpful. Okay, let's go get him. And no shooting if you can help it. God forbid you accidentally put a bullet through his head."

Up above them Titus had rounded a huge rock, temporarily disappearing from sight. Doc picked up the pace, with Eustace following, his Winchester out but his finger free of the trigger, his hand wrapped around the barrel just in front of the guard.

Cactus, yucca, and agave were beginning to give way to greasewood and sagebrush with little grass—and that in evidence, dried and yellowed by the sun. They closed the gap separating them from Titus and when he reappeared he was less than a hundred feet ahead. Hearing their horses, he spurred his own.

"Hold it!" called Doc. "Stop where you are or you're dead!"

Eustace fired twice over his head. Titus ducked. For a split second Doc thought he had been hit; he seemed to slump forward. But then he straightened in his saddle, reined about, and came toward them, his hands upraised.

"What's this about? What do you want?"

"Erland Titus?" asked Doc.

Titus's face fell. "Who are you?"

Doc showed his I.D. card. "Pinkerton National Detective Agency."

"Pink . . ."

"Operatives Hillbank and Weatherbee." He waved the warrant secured in Baptist Wells. "You're under arrest. We're taking you back."

"Arrest for what?"

"Conspiracy. You were in on the robbery."

"If you're talking about my bank, you're crazy. That's a stinking lie!"

"If it is, you'll get your chance to prove it."

"You think I was in on it just because I left town? It's not so. I left for personal reasons."

"Hand over your gun, thumb and forefinger on the hilt." Doc spurred his horse forward to take the weapon.

"Sure, sure, anything you say. But see here, can't we talk this over? I can explain."

"Hold it right there, boys. Toss down the hardware!"

Doc and Eustace turned slowly. Doc's heart fell in his chest. Two men were standing atop the huge rock they had circled, bringing Titus back into sight. Two rifles were high and aimed—at him, at Eustace.

"What the hell," began Eustace.

"Shut up," said Doc wearily.

"We're Pinkerton detectives, damn it!" bellowed Eustace.

"You can't hold us up, it's against the law. Can't you see you're interfering with an arrest?"

Doc groaned, hung his head, and fleetingly thought of Job and his travail.

"Eustace, just shut up and do as the man says."

"Listen to your dude pal, sonny boy," said the older of the two, the tips of his frazzled mustache lifting slightly as his homely face broke into a grin. "He's making good sense."

"Who are they?" whispered Titus.

"You're asking me?" asked Doc, opening his jacket to show that he was unarmed. Eustace swore under his breath and dropped the rifle and his gunbelt and .45.

"Cut the small talk, you two. You with the slouch hat, turn around and keep on heading up the trail. You two follow him and no tricks. We'd as lief blow all three o' your heads off as wink an eye. Keep that in mind."

Less than a quarter mile into the hills the profusion of boulders and outcroppings began to thin, giving way to a shallow valley in the center of which stood a number of dilapidated buildings confronting each other in two long lines down either side of a broad street. Weeds and grass flourished along its full length. A ghost town. They had come nearly thirty miles from Blacktower by Doc's estimate.

"Welcome to Blacktower, boys," said the younger of their captors, a kid in his teens, trying very hard to create the impression that he was a man. But his high-pitched voice and cheeks that had never felt a razor combined to frustrate the effort. The three of them questioned his statement with their eyes.

"This is the o-riginal Blacktower," explained his companion. "The one you know is a come-lately town. This here's been abandoned for years."

"What do you want with us?" Doc asked for the sixth time, having yet to elicit a response.

"You got it backwards, friend," said the older man. "It ain't what we want with you, it's what you want with us."

"You tell 'em, Rafe," laughed the boy, slapping his knee, sending his horse lunging forward.

"You was coming for us, mister, an' you sure enough found us."

"You're mistaken," said Doc evenly. "We were looking for Mr. Titus here. We don't have the slightest interest in you or your friends or the o-riginal Blacktower."

"You're a damn liar! We'll find out what you want, don't make no mistake about that." Rafe paused, his brow furrowing. "Did he say Titus, Justin?"

"That's what he said."

"You know someone by that name?" asked the banker, his facial muscles tightening. Doc was less than ten feet from him, but he still could not tell whether his expression was one of apprehension or concealed relief. Erland Titus was a cagy one, he decided, not nearly as soft as his newspaper picture suggested; he was tough; he had grit and extraordinary determination. Any man prepared to risk reputation and hide on the sort of mission he had undertaken had to have both in quantity.

Rafe ignored him, instead exchanging glances with the boy. It was all the answer Titus needed. My, my, thought Doc. Journey's end. Mr. Banker is about to be reunited with Mrs. Banker, although "reunited" was hardly the word. His beloved Ellie belonged to another now, whether or not he was willing to admit it. Still, what choice did he have? What a fool's errand he had set for himself, poor man. From the look on his face he seemed to be thinking precisely that. He had taken off his false beard, stuffing it in his jacket pocket, part of it hanging out foolishly. Bits of spirit gum still clung to his cheeks and chin.

They were riding down the weed-infested street. Justin spurred his horse on, then reined up and jumped nimbly down. He tethered to a hitch rack, one end of which had come loose and now lay on the ground, effectively symbolizing the ramshackle entirety of the town. They watched the boy enter a building—a bank, according to the six-foot sign standing on its end alongside the door.

"Inside, you three," said Rafe, motioning with his rifle.

They assembled in the front room. Doc glanced about, as did Eustace. Erland Titus gasped.

"Recognize where you are?" asked Rafe. "In your bank." He laughed raucously. "It's yours, all right, different building, that's all."

Not entirely Titus's bank; only about two-thirds. The remainder was the original Blacktower Bank. The vault door taken from Baptist Wells stood at the right rear, set into a newly constructed sandstone and mortar vault.

Three men emerged from a back room on the opposite side. At once Doc recognized Mr. Stetson. The little man was resting his head from his outsized hat, but was wearing everything else he had had on the night of the disagreement in Poindexter's. He had killed twenty-one people in cold blood and had gotten away with it, at least so far. Doc was convinced he was the culprit; he had never seen such vicious hatred in human eyes as those of the little man as he backed through the swinging doors that night.

He came swaggering up to Doc, raising himself on tiptoe and thrusting his face up close. He squinted astigmatically.

"I know you." He turned to the others. "I seen him before. Where 'bouts we meet up, huh?"

"I don't recall the pleasure," said Doc quietly.

"In town, that's where." He ran a hand down Doc's lapel. "How come you wear them fancy duds? You an actor, drummer? You a cardsharper?"

"He's a Pinkerton detective, Wallace," said Rafe.

Wallace reacted. "I'll be a son of a bitch! What in hell you doing, bringing him here?"

"He ain't the half of it," said Rafe. "This here one's the banker from Baptist Wells. In the flesh. Come to get his missus and his money back." He laughed. The others joined in. One of Wallace's companions who had come out of the back room with him was built like a coil of spring steel, mused Doc, sizing him up: stocky, solid sinew, bull neck, arms like railroad ties, and a slender

beard roping down his cheeks to a knot at the point of his
chin. He looked powerful enough to lift the vault door and
set it in place with his bare hands. The other man was six
inches taller, but looked consumptive, his narrow shoulders slumped, his chest concave. He coughed lightly, per-
sistently into the back of his hand, heightening the suspicion
in Doc's mind that he was not well.

"I ask you again," snapped Wallace, confronting Rafe,
scowling up at him, the heels of his hands hard against his
pistol grips. "Why'd you bring 'em here? Answer me!"

"It was either that or gun 'em down," said Justin
timidly. "We figured the boss'd want to see the banker
here."

"You figured. You simple-minded little asshole, you
ain't got brains enough to figure nothing!"

"Simmer down, Wallace," said the muscular man beside him. He had a high-pitched voice, higher even than
Wallace's shrill chirp. A small voice.

Discussion began over what to do with the three prisoners.
Wallace called the muscular one Scofe, for Scofield, decided Doc; his consumptive-looking sidekick was Hobie.
Doc, Eustace, and Titus stood listening while the five
outlaws debated their fate.

"You shoulda gunned 'em down up in the hills," declared Wallace a second and a third time. Hobie agreed,
but the others weren't altogether sure.

Scofield offered a suggestion. "I say we toss 'em in the
jug till the boss gets back."

The others, with the exception of Wallace, agreed. The
little man was out for blood and made no effort to disguise
it.

"Why the hell do that?" he sputtered irritably. "Then
we got to feed 'em, fetch 'em water. He won't be back till
who knows when. Why put it off? I say we march 'em
outside, line 'em up, gun 'em down, and dump 'em in a
hole. Scofe, Justin, go fetch shovels and a pick."

Scofe and Justin hesitated, glancing at the others in turn
questioningly.

"Move!" barked Wallace.

They stood out back. A breeze was up, bending the grass, whipping against loose shutters, sending tumbleweeds rolling about. The sun was dying over the rim of the hills, searing the rock with its crimson fire, sending soft, velvety shadows spilling over the land. Doc and Titus were handed shovels, Eustace, the pick.

"Get to digging," growled Wallace, standing hands on hips, surveying them. "Dig one big hole. It'll serve."

"That ain't right, Wallace," interposed Scofield. "It ain't Christian. Man's entitled to his own private grave, not to be piled in with others."

"He's right, Wallace," said Rafe. Hobie nodded agreement. Justin offered no comment; he was preoccupied watching a yellow butterfly flit lightly from one ruby-red agave rosette to another.

"I'm in charge while Ben's away. What I say goes. One hole."

They began digging. Like water in a pot on a stove, Doc's hatred for the little loudmouth with the big clothes and the massive burden of insecurity had been simmering and now broke into a boil. So tightly did he grip the handle of his shovel, his knuckles showed white. His disgust and frustration also revealed itself in his expression, despite a conscious effort to keep from betraying it. Wallace sidled up to him.

"You'd like to swing that shovel, wouldn't you, Mr. Pink. Like to chop my head off. Look at him, boys, he's mad as a pony with a wasp up its ass. Go ahead, Pink, swing it, swing that shovel."

"Leave him alone," said Scofield.

The expression on his face said clearly that he had no liking for this, for what was to come. None of them did. But Wallace was reveling in it, grinning, chuckling, continuing to goad Doc, insisting he swing the shovel.

"Chop my pumpkin head off. I dare you. Do it, go ahead. You'll see, I'll gun you down before you can get it 'bove your shoulder. Try me, go ahead."

"Shut up, Wallace," burst out Hobie.

Wallace looked from one face to another, seeing enough

to persuade him to bridle his tongue. Doc relaxed his grip slightly, but the boiling went on.

He dug and flung dirt. This he hated, he thought, even more than his little antagonist. Blades chunked softly into the sandy ground as the three of them worked on in silence. Doc examined his feelings. He had never harbored what one might term an abject fear of death, the sort of dread that wrenched one out of a nightmare and lifted you up in bed, panting, sweating, your heart hammering the wall of your chest. Regarding death, his own, he was philosophical. This figured. It was an attitude that came with the territory. In this line, certainly in the field, one lived by his wits and his gun, taking chances as they came, as they were thrust upon you. Survival was a precious and all too frequently elusive commodity. He and Raider had managed to survive, inviting, encountering, and avoiding death too often, gradually reducing the odds.

Still, dying in a shoot-out was one thing; being executed by these low-lifes, particularly the runt, was disgusting, intolerable, an affront to decency. Outrageous, maddening! Stop time for five seconds, he thought, freeze them in place, let him indeed swing his shovel. And slice all their heads off. The tumbleweeds continued their aimless wandering; he pictured five heads rolling about.

He didn't mind dying. No, that he couldn't say, not in honesty. Anyone who said such a thing was either a liar or a fool, or overcome by a conviction too powerful to deal with rationally, in the manner of a religious fanatic seduced by the prospect of martyrdom. What he minded, what he despised was his utter helplessness in preventing the runt from gunning them down in cold blood, grinning sadistically, laughing them into unconsciousness. He had no plans to die a hero when his time arrived, but to leave this life ignominiously, the prospect of it, was speedily becoming unbearable. To be pitched into a common grave like starved cattle . . .

"What you thinking about, Pink?" Wallace's high, grating voice shattered his thoughts. "I'll tell you what you should be thinking about, what you're going to be leaving behind: good booze, good pals, the feel o' the sun warm on your face, the prettiness all around you, women. So soft, comfortable, their arms around you, your cock pounding deep. Big, warm tits bouncing and jouncing, that old hard nipple under your tongue. You married, Pink? Look at him, boys, he is for sure. You thinking about her, Pink? Thinking about lying with your skin warm against hers?"

"Shut up, Wallace!" said Scofield. "Leave him alone."

"Who in hell you think you're talking to, lamebrain?"

"You, you little shit!"

Wallace stiffened, his eyes blazing, his hand stealing toward his right gun. Call him every vile name in the dirty dictionary, thought Doc, looking on, but never little. Uttering the mere word in his presence must be like a straight razor slicing up his spine.

The two glared at each other, their hands on their guns. Hobie stepped between them.

"Cut it out. You, Pink, keep shoveling."

They had opened the hole to a depth of two feet. Titus, breathing hard from a combination of effort and nervousness, paused to mop his face with his handkerchief. Wallace confronted him.

"Too bad about you, banker. Crying shame, that's what it is. You ain't going to be around long enough to say hello to your missus." He laughed. "Not that she wants to see you, you can bet. She's all wrapped up in Ben. She's his mind and body. She don't want you. Doesn't need you nohow."

Scofield cursed and rushed to his side, grabbing him by the shoulder, spinning him around.

"You son of a bitch, you shut your mouth and keep it shut!" He pushed Wallace in the chest, shoving him back a step. The little man jerked out his guns, sputtering loudly, his face rapidly reddening.

"You bastard, I'll—"

It was as far as he got. Scofield swung, smashing him full in the jaw, toppling him. Eustace cheered. Doc glared at him, silently mouthing shut up. Wallace lay stretched out cold. Scofield picked him up like a small child and carried him off between two of the buildings, disappearing from sight.

"He asked for it," observed Rafe to Justin.

"He maybe asked for it," said Hobie, "but when he comes around he's going to raise red hell. Somebody better hide his six-guns. Goddamn little wart, if he wasn't Ben's brother he'da got his block knocked off by every one o' us long afore now."

"Fellows is all the time taking pokes at him on account o' his big mouth and nasty talk," said Justin, nodding vigorous agreement with his own words.

"Keep digging," said Rafe.

Doc started, then stopped. "Rafe, can I say something?"

Scofield was coming back, a dour look spread across his face, his eyes narrowed and filled with worry.

"I laid him on his bed. He'll be out for a half hour."

"You shouldn'ta done it, Scofe," said Hobie, shaking his head.

"He had it coming. For long as I've known him."

"That he did, but you shouldn'ta."

"I'm fed to the eyes with him and his wiseacre ways. He's loco." He looked at the others, asking with his eyes for nods of agreement. He got one from Rafe. "Poisoning people, just 'cause they laugh at him. He's sicker in the head than a damn goat. We four are stupid to hang around here. He's going to get every mother's son of us hanged if we don't hobble him."

"Bullshit," said Rafe, spitting, wetly registering his refusal to accept this. "Ain't nobody living's going to hang this old boy. What we're doing ain't no hanging offense. Besides, they got to catch us first. Got to find us."

"These three didn't have no trouble finding us," said Hobie.

"They didn't find shit. Rafe and the lad led 'em straight back here." Scofield glanced at Doc, then at Titus. "You wouldn't be digging now if the two of 'em'd left you alone."

"Our job is to protect this place," said Rafe self-consciously. "Keep strangers from nosing round. We done our job the way we should."

"Can I say something?" Doc repeated.

"What?" asked Scofield.

"One question. What is killing us going to do for you?"

"Hell, that ought to be clear as day," said Scofield. "With you outta the way, we get to keep our secret. We got business going here we'd prefer folks outside shouldn't know anything about, except for certain parties."

"You're juggling hot money."

"Our business is none o' yours," snapped Rafe. "Dig!"

"Just one more thing," said Doc, gesturing for indulgence. "Something you might give serious thought to. Up to now you four are wanted for bank robbery, that's all. You shoot us, even stand by and let Wallace do it, it automatically makes you accomplices. When they hang him, they'll hang you right along with him. Depend on it. Be smart, Scofield."

"I'm smart enough. We got you, and you're dead, with nobody out there the wiser."

"I'm not the only operative in the area."

"I'm here," said Eustace proudly.

Doc cut him off with an icy stare. "There are Pinkertons swarming all over. The Santa Fe Railroad hired the agency to find that payroll. Sooner or later . . ."

"We'll take care o' your friends when they show," said Rafe calmly. "*If* they show."

They resumed digging. Presently—within seconds, it seemed to Doc—they had lowered the hole to six feet. He and Eustace stood at the bottom, tossing up shovelfuls, while Titus, stripped to the waist, bathed with sweat, pale and beginning to tremble, stood topside, clearing dirt from the edge.

"That'll do," said Scofield. He nodded to Titus. "You can get down in now. Let me give you a hand."

Doc had to grit his teeth to keep from convulsing with laughter. A man being helped down into his grave by his prospective murderer. Priceless!

All three stood looking up at their captors. To a man, the outlaws' faces expressed distaste for what was to come. Very slowly, Scofield eased his six-guns from their holsters.

"You boys got to understand one thing," he said solemnly. "There's nothing personal in this."

"That's comforting to know," said Doc brightly.

"Shut your mouth!" Scofield softened his tone. "What I mean is we don't hate you or nothing. We're not like Wallace, none of us. Hell, nobody is. It's just, we got to protect ourselves. You understand."

"Sure," said Eustace, understandingly. Again Doc shot him a glare, so icy, Eustace very nearly winced.

Scofield knelt at the edge. He licked his lips nervously. He frowned. He took a deep breath and let it out slowly. He holstered his weapons.

"Okay, Rafe, it's time."

Rafe came up to him, a dumbfounded look on his face. "What you putting away your irons for?"

"You can do the honors."

"Not me."

"The hell not you! You haul and shoot 'em, you damn chicken liver!"

"Nothing chicken-livered 'bout it. You're the one decided. You said time. Pulled your guns to do it an' everything. So, go ahead."

In the distance there came the muffled sound of galloping hooves. All four looked off toward the lowering clouds, their bellies stained soft pink by the vanished sun.

"It's Ben and her," said Justin.

Two horses came pounding up. On one was a tall, broad-shouldered, dark-eyed man, neatly attired entirely in black, save for his silver gunbelt and the studs on his boots. With him was an arrestingly beautiful woman. Her jet-black hair tumbled to her shoulders; her silk-figured shirt was filled to bursting with her pride; she had a slender waist and the imperious look of a queen. She carried a riding crop. She had an exquisite mouth, thought Doc, staring up at her: full-lipped, sensuous, deliciously inviting. She smiled coldly.

"Hello, Erland."

"El . . ."

Doc half laughed to himself. Small wonder the people in Blacktower to whom he'd described Ellie Titus had been unable to place her. They'd never seen her as a blonde. If they'd seen her at all.

"Mr. Titus," said the man. "Ben Hungerford's the name." He squatted down and extended his hand in greeting. "A pleasure to meet you."

Titus ignored his hand.

Hungerford shrugged, glanced at his hand, closed it, and straightened, addressing Scofield. "Where's Wally?"

"In his room. Him and me had a little run-in."

"You hit him."

"Ben, I took all I could take."

"No need to explain. I know my brother better than you." He gestured toward the hole. "Are you going to bury these boys alive, or did you plan to shoot them first?"

"Shoot 'em," said Rafe.

Ben pulled off his gloves and, turning his back to the hole, retraced his steps to Mrs. Titus's side.

"Get on with it, then."

"Sure, boss," said Hobie. He was holding a Winchester; he levered a cartridge into the chamber, raised the rifle, and aimed at Titus.

"Wait!" burst Mrs. Titus.

She seized Hungerford by the sleeve and walked him a few steps farther away out of earshot. Doc glanced at the banker. The dread masking his face, draining it of color, appeared to give way to a hopeful expression. He was holding his breath, curling and uncurling his fingers.

"Sweetheart, I can't do that," said Hungerford in a tone that appealed for understanding. "If we let him go, we've got to let the other two. It wouldn't be fair not to. We've got to be fair. We can't play favorites. You see that, don't you, honey?"

They went on discussing it, lowering their voices to

below everyone else's hearing. Doc's eyes deserted Titus for Eustace. The boy was taking it all with remarkable calm. Not a flicker of emotion showed in his eyes. He wasn't worried, he wasn't smiling, his mind was either emptied of all thoughts or miles away. Probably with Florry-Mae, decided Doc.

Hungerford came back to them, squatting a second time. "You're in luck, boys. It seems the lady and I have reached an impasse. You're a fortunate fellow, Erland. She's very protective. Loyal as they come, yes, sir."

Titus's face failed to acknowledge either that he was fortunate or that he could agree that his wife was loyal. The three of them were helped up and out of the grave; suddenly no longer a grave, reflected Doc, dusting off his trousers and sighing inwardly, merely a hole in the ground. Whether they were ever to be buried there, however, remained to be seen.

"Better to live on a hook than not at all," he said quietly.

"You say something, Doc?" asked Eustace.

"He's no doubt talking to his maker," said Hungerford, laughing.

Wallace appeared, emerging from between the buildings. His jaw was swollen; he touched it gingerly with his fingertips. Sighting Scofield, he glared venomously and came striding toward him.

"Take it easy, Wally," said his brother.

"Son of a bitch hit me!"

"You asked for it," said Scofield tersely.

"Cut it out, both of you," said Hungerford. "Rafe, Hobie, get these boys into a cell. You, Hobie, keep an eye on them."

"What the hell you talking about, cell?" said Wallace. "They got to be shot. Them two are Pinkertons. They're out to get us proper." He reached for his guns. "They're dead, goddamn it!"

"Hold it!" said Hobie, standing to one side of the little man and leveling his rifle at his head.

Wallace's brother smiled benignly. "Put your guns away, Wally. There's no need to worry about them. I promise you, they're not going to do us any harm."

"You're wrong, Ben. Damn it, man, what's got into you?"

"That's enough! Do as I tell you. You and Hobie put them in a cell."

Pouting, grumbling to himself, Wallace joined Hobie, ushering the prisoners down between the buildings, down the street to the left and into a time- and weather-battered sheriff's office. The front door hung by one hinge. The wind had come up in earnest, speeding the tumbleweeds, raising dust, setting it swirling. Hobie caught some in his eye.

"Goddamn it to hell!" He stood grinding his knuckles into his eye, filling it with blood, continuing to swear, eliciting a laugh from Wallace. He pushed Eustace bodily inside. Doc could see that he had it in for the boy in particular; the little man's two Colts made him as tall as Eustace, in his estimation, at least. Doc cast a sidelong glance at the boy as he was shoved up alongside him. No reaction to Wallace's abuse showed on Eustace's face. Hobie and Wallace clumped along over the bare floor behind them. Doc surveyed the interior. To the right stood a desk, its curtain top closed. Around back, three spindle chairs stood about. A Neale & Urban safe door with its characteristic right-hand lock, panoramic scene, twin handles, and decorated edging stood leaning against the far wall, the safe it had originally been attached to nowhere in evidence. A map of the Llano Estacado was tacked to the wall above the door, speckled with pinholes and covered with hand-written notations. There was an Illinois Fire Insurance Company calendar dated fourteen years earlier, and to the right of the entrance to the cell area hung an empty rifle rack. A key ring hung from its peg beside it. There were four small cells, two on either side of a small walkway. Wallace tried to reach the key ring, stretching his arm as high as he could, coming within two inches of it.

"Don't just stand there," he barked to Hobie. "Get down the keys!"

Doc bit back a grin. Eustace tried to, but was unsuccessful. Wallace bristled.

"What the hell's so funny, you!"

"Nothing."

Rearing back, Wallace drove his fist hard into Eustace's kidneys. Eustace grunted, bent, straightened, snapping back upward, shoved his arms out left and right, and began whirling. His left caught Hobie squarely in the temple, knocking him flat, the key ring jingling down on top of him. His right barely cleared Wallace's head, came around a second time a foot lower and slammed him in the chest. Hobie stirred, groaning, shaking out the cobwebs, holding the side of his head with one hand, groping for his rifle with the other. Doc and Titus gasped, watching transfixed as Eustace picked Wallace up bodily, lifted him above his head and hurled him at Hobie. Wallace flew over Hobie's head and pounded against the wall alongside the desk. Whirling about, Eustace made for the door and was out before Hobie could raise, aim, and fire. Two wild shots sped Eustace on his way. Doc tensed. Hobie swung the rifle around, moving his aim slowly back and forth between him and Titus.

"Either o' you takes one step toward the door and you're dead."

He got to his feet, scowling, shaking away the dizziness. Wallace groaned but continued to lay without moving.

"Inside," growled Hobie, gesturing with the rifle and retrieving the key ring. He locked them in a cell and went back to Wallace. Standing at the bars, Doc and Titus could see most of the office. The little man was sitting up, holding his head with both hands. Scofield and Justin came running in.

"We heard shots," began Scofield. "What the . . .?"

"The big one jumped us. I think Wallace is hurt bad."

Scofield grinned. "Ain't that a shame!"

Justin blanched. "The big one got away. That's bad."

"You boys get after him," snapped Hobie. "He'll be headin' back where he come from for sure."

"He didn't take no horse," said Justin. "We'da heard."

"Stop jawing and move! If he gets away, Ben'll have our hides."

Scofield and Justin fled. Doc heard them ride off seconds later. Hobie had picked Wallace up and was helping him out the door. Doc moved to the rear of the cell, sitting down wearily on one of the two crude wooden bunks. No mattress, no blanket, only a frame with a dozen slats set crosswise.

"You think he'll make it?" Titus asked.

Doc shrugged. "I don't know how far he'll get without a horse."

"Amazing. I jumped a foot I was so surprised. He exploded, pinwheeling like that."

Doc smirked. "Wallace made a big mistake. His brother's going to love this."

"God bless him, I hope the boy makes it."

"Cross your fingers. He may surprise us. All of us. He's not very quick. He's awkward, clumsy, doesn't know his own strength. Strength is about all he's got, that and a sort of primitive resourcefulness. He just might be able to stay out of their way until dark. He'll be safe then. He can walk to Blacktower."

"He really isn't overly bright, is he? I couldn't help noticing."

"Not overly."

"Have you two been partners long?"

"We just teamed up. You're our first case. I was with another fellow for years, a farmer from Arkansas." Doc shook his head slowly, a nostalgic expression taking hold, memory recounting the days and weeks before Eustace. "Fellow by the name of Raider."

"Another Eustace?"

"On the contrary. Smartest man I think I've ever known. Not educated—just about able to read and write, actually— but shrewd. Horse sense like you've never seen. Trail sense. He had the instincts of an Indian or an old-time trapper. And he was at his best when the going got rough. I've never met anybody like him, the way he handled himself under fire. Coolest man alive. A man and a half, that's Raider.''

"You split up?''

"The agency split us up. At times we had disagreements. It got a trifle hectic.''

Titus grinned. "You got along like two wildcats in a gunnysack.''

"Good analogy.''

"Where is he now?''

Doc shrugged. "Working somewhere with a new partner.'' For a long moment he was silent, wrapped in reverie. Suddenly he slapped his knee and shot to his feet.

"Ancient history. Here *we* are. Reprieve from the governor.''

"You think it's only temporary?''

"I'm afraid so. Still, if it hadn't been for your wife, it wouldn't be that.''

"Mr. Weatherbee, if it hadn't been for my wife none of this would be happening. I'd be back in Baptist Wells working, she'd be home getting dinner ready, you and Eustace would be on another case.''

"True. All the same, she did save our lives.''

"Temporarily, you think.''

"Let me put it this way, as long as she's around, we're okay, but if she leaves again, if she and Hungerford go riding off, don't be surprised if we have callers. The instant the two of them are out of sight.''

"You're assuming . . .''

"I'm not. Think about it, Hungerford can't afford to let us live. There's too much at stake.''

"But if his men kill us, how would he explain it to Ellie?''

"Erland, that would be the easiest part. However he explains it, whether she buys it or doesn't, it won't do us any good.''

"Ellie, Ellie, Ellie." Titus sat down slowly on the bunk opposite. "I deserve the palm for being the world's biggest fool. You know something, self-delusion is like a disease. It infects you, spreads through your system, just takes over. There's no way to knock it out. You don't even try. *I* never have.

"Men like me should never marry women like Ellie. It was wrong from the start. We both knew that."

"You loved each other, didn't you?"

"We thought we did. I know I loved her, passionately. But that doesn't change anything, doesn't help matters. It's what hurts, actually. It's the core of one's self-delusion. She's got a devil in her. She can't help it, she was born with it. She needs danger, excitement, fire in her life like others need food and water. She can't exist without the spice. Marrying me was a horrendous mistake. To me, banking is exciting. To most people, it's dull as dishwater. Dry, dusty, routinized, boring. It made me boring. Ellie loathed banking. It's my life, and she despised it. Women like her want what men like me can never give them."

"If what you say is true, why did she ever marry you in the first place?"

"She didn't. I married her. There's a difference, you see. I did the chasing, the persuading, I talked her into it. I promised her the moon, with every intention of delivering, mind you. She bought it lock, stock, and barrel. One day she woke up to the discovery that I couldn't give her a blessed thing, beyond what money can buy. Certainly not what she really wants, not what a man like Hungerford can give her."

"Hungerford can get her a rope around her lovely neck."

"Ah, but that's exactly what she craves, don't you see? Not to be hanged, of course, but the excitement, the danger, the risk. It nourishes something in her soul, her spirit. She can't live without it."

"With all due respect, Erland, I think you're making excuses for her."

Titus had been talking to the floor, his elbows on his

knees, his chin planted between his fists. He looked up slowly, his cornflower blue eyes finding Doc's eyes and riveting them.

"Why shouldn't I make excuses? She's my wife. I love her."

CHAPTER TWELVE

Disgust settled over Raider like a fog of foul odor. The case was going poorly, and up to now there hadn't been thirty minutes put together at any one time that he could look back upon and say he enjoyed. Outside of the shoot-out. To this state of affairs he could add Algernon. In his relentless posturing, his unabating pretense to nobility, he had developed into a royal pain in the ass. He was such an old lady, reflected Raider ruefully, sitting in a rickity chair on two legs on the verandah of the Hotel Blodgett, his feet up on the railing. Such a goddamn stickler for details. Him and his little black book, always scribbling in it or in the case journal. As if they'd come up with anything worth putting into the report. All that should go in were the bones, anyway: chased bad guys, caught up with same, shoot-out, three dead, four captured, case closed.

He used to think Doc was by the book to a fare-thee-well. Algernon was making him look downright sloppy. Why in hell didn't people like that stick to clerking in a countinghouse, where details mattered, where a comma out of place was enough to shake up the whole shooting match? Why did they take on work that called for more off-the-cuff decisions and shooting from the hip than any fifty jobs? Were all Englishmen like Algernon, he wondered? If they were, the damn country must be in a hell of a fix, grinding along like an overloaded train, up to their ears in bullshit, busting each other's balls, pointing out mistakes.

Doc. Where had the grinning son of a bitch gotten to? Him and Wagner's nephew. What was he up to? Was he okay?

He missed him. Every time he looked at Algernon, a little bit more. Not that Algernon was the worst of the litter, the loudest, the nastiest, the orneriest. What it came right down to was his biggest fault of all, one that he could hardly blame him for: the fact that he wasn't Doc Weatherbee and as a substitute was what anyone else would be—a miserable failure.

An elderly man clad in a well-tailored black cassimere suit, carrying an ivory-headed walking stick and hiding his hair under a Danbury stiff fur hat that looked like a flat-rimmed cuspidor turned upside down, was coming up the steps.

"Say, brother," asked Raider. "You got the time o' day?"

The man started, his handsome face clouding. Clearing his throat, he hauled forth a watch the size of a baseball. "Five minutes past four."

"Jesus Christ!" Raider shot to his feet, the chair clattering to rest behind him.

"I beg your pardon, sir?"

"Not you, not you, not you. Him, him. Thanks, thanks."

The man stared in puzzlement, thrust out his walking stick, and followed it into the hotel. Raider followed him.

Algernon was in the room, drinking tea, his little alcohol stove bubbling merrily.

"I knew it," sighed Raider.

"What's the matter?"

"It's past time we went back out, that's what's the matter!"

"Really, old chap, you must know perfectly well by this time that four o'clock is tea time. Give me two more minutes and we'll be on our merry way."

"How come you always got to drink that crap exactly on the dot at four? What if you don't? What if you're early or late? What happens, do you turn into a goddamn pumpkin?"

Algernon laughed. "I say, that's clever. Turn into a pumpkin."

"If you write it down in your little black book, I'll kill you."

"You've made a joke and you don't even realize it. Seriously, the reason we English drink our tea on the dot is because it was ever thus. Tradition, old boy. Tea is more than a beverage, it's a bloody institution, like the monarchy, the hunt, and the Bard. As an Englishman's home is his castle, his tea is the emblem of his uniqueness in the family of man, as it were. On second thought, tea drinking is more than an institution, adherence to tradition, a patriotic duty. It is, dare I say it, something of a religious observance."

"Good, fine."

"Please, I'm not finished."

"The hell you're not. Drink up, for Chrissakes. We got to get back out. Tonight we're staying out. We're getting out too far to bother coming all the way in."

"I thought the original plan was to move on to the next town?"

"It was, now it's not. Combing the area makes more sense. Huggens and his boys covered a circle all the way out to five miles. We already better than doubled that."

"How far out do you plan on going? To the Texas border, Mexico?"

Algernon finished his tea and began washing his cup and saucer in the basin. Raider blew out the flame under the alcohol pan.

"Believe me, I know we're doing this the hard way. I know there's a good chance nothing'll come of it. If you can think of a better plan, I'll listen."

"Towns, Raider, settlements where people reside. Communities are natural magnets for the areas surrounding them. Whatever goes on outside of a town, whoever lives or works or steals or murders either eventually finds his way to town or news of what he does finds its way. Questioning people can be extraordinarily useful. And where are the people? Not wandering around out on the plains."

"Maybe you're right."

"Certainly, I'm right. Have you ever known me to be wrong?"

"Closest town to here is on the tracks: Sowville. I hear it's so small you can practically tuck it into the lobby downstairs."

"Sowville it is, then. Shall we be off?" He started for the door, stopped, and turned. "Tell me something. Where on earth do they get some of these names: Pole City, Glory, Sowville. Where are your Queensborough-in-Sheppey, Saltburn and Marske-by-the-Sea, Dalton-in-Furness, Epping, Debighshire?"

"We left them over in England when we lit out back when."

They rode toward Sowville, fifty miles to the west, deserting the Santa Fe tracks, following a pencil line on Raider's map loaned him by Marshal Huggens. They had stopped in to see the marshal before leaving. He and his deputies hadn't gotten as far as Sowville, not a tenth of the distance, electing instead to ride their ever-widening circle. In Huggen's opinion, the projected one-hundred-mile round trip to the next town down the line promised a wild goose chase. He insisted that anybody wanted did not light out for a town, chiefly because towns were connected by telegraph wires. Deserted shacks on the plains and in the hills were bereft of such modern conveniences.

The marshal had gotten out wanted dodgers on the suspect, his daughter drawing a likeness of the little man, guided by the two bartenders' detailed description of him. Huggens gave a dodger to Raider, wishing the two of them good hunting as he did so.

The sun was slipping below the horizon, the shadows lengthening like enormous, endless drapes laid out on the Llano Estacado to dry. The air was becoming chilly. On they rode.

To the northwest on their right, Eustace dropped to his knees, duck-waddling backwards under the cover of a boulder wedged partway down into a ravine. He gulped for boulder wedged partway down into a ravine. He gulped for air, his chest heaving, perspiration pouring down him. Peering out of his hiding place and across the shadow of the bluffs of the Llano Estacado, he could see the plain beckoning. Beyond it, farther than his eyes could see, lay Blacktower.

He considered his situation and resolved to stay put, get his wind, restore his strength as best he could, wait for darkness, and pray that the few clouds trafficking the sky overhead would increase in number, join, and cover the moon and the stars.

He caught his breath and held it. He could hear loose rock clattering, a horse neigh, hooves, voices calling out. Familiar voices . . .

"This way, damn it, he musta gone down here. It's the only way through."

Crouching lower, Eustace backed deeper into the shadow of the rock.

CHAPTER THIRTEEN

"I miss Judith," said Doc dolefully.

"Your wife?"

"My mule."

"Oh . . ."

"She's in good hands, thank the Lord, in the livery stable in Blacktower. But I know she misses me dreadfully. No stranger can pamper her like I do. She likes me to pick over her oats for her before she's served. She's a picky eater. Has to have her water just the right temperature, not too cold."

"Do you think Eustace got through?"

"They haven't brought him back, though I don't imagine they would if they do catch him. Getting through the hills shouldn't be too hard. He can hear them before they get too close. The hardest part'll be crossing the plains. If I were Hungerford I'd send two men out a hundred fifty yards apart, riding straight as the crow flies to Blacktower."

"If Eustace uses his head, he'll circle. He won't head straight back."

"Eustace is Eustace, Erland. I told you before, his mind isn't his strong suit. Unfortunately for us, Hungerford's appears to be."

Doc stood up. "I'm hungry. I wonder if they're planning on feeding us? I should have reminded Hobie. Condemned man's supposed to eat a hearty meal."

"I wish you wouldn't talk like that."

"Sorry. I talk too much, so Raider always tells me."

He gripped the bars in the little window seven feet up from the floor. One was slightly loose at the base. Working it back and forth, he might be able to free it, pull it loose from the top, he thought. Why bother? Even if he managed to loosen all three, the window was much too small to squeeze through. He pulled over his bunk and, standing on the corner, peered out. It was pitch black outside, so dark he couldn't even make out the wall of the building next door. He listened. Somebody laughed, then all was quiet.

"Can you see anything?" asked Titus.

"The future. Sorry, I'm still talking too much."

He got down, returned his bunk to its corner, and sat down on the edge. Titus was lying down, his coat off, his hands behind his head.

"How do you think they work this 'business,' as Rafe calls it?" Doc asked. "What s Hungerford up to? Why the elaborate charade, restoring the   and all? I don't see any customers flocking into town."

"The sort of customers he's looking   don't flock. I'm sure people come here. Federal currency carries serial numbers, as you know. Since the war, more and more local communities have gotten out of the business of printing their own money. Washington's dollar has become the nation's dollar, even out here in the territories. It's backed by gold. That's better than a man's word."

"So when somebody steals money from a bank . . ."

"The bank has a list of the serial numbers. If whoever runs off with it tries to spend it elsewhere, they may succeed, but sooner or later it finds its way through a cashier's window at the local bank. It's traced back, and if the thieves are still in the area, even if they're not, if they're still in the country, they'd better run and hide. My guess is stolen money is brought here, Hungerford 'buys' it, literally, charging an exorbitant fee for his services, to be sure, carries it out of the country, and swaps it for U.S. currency. Clean currency."

"Mexico?"

"Probably Monterrey."

"Brings the money all the way down there, exchanges it, and brings back clean money."

"Exactly. Only one thing puzzles me." Titus made a face and scratched his cheek, thoughtfully.

"Setting up an actual, physical banking facility to carry out the operation?" queried Doc.

"No, you can charge that up to his sense of humor, or possibly a passion for the legitimate. After all, he already had part of a bank, he just needed to complete it. No, I'm thinking of the location. We must be nearly three hundred and fifty miles from the border."

"From El Paso, easily."

"Why not set the thing up down there? Someplace close to the border."

"Probably because it's too risky. If the law starts looking for him, along the border is the most logical place. Better to put up with the inconvenience of distance." Doc's face expressed admiration. "What a lovely setup. He can carry a million in large bills. He can ride to Tucumcari, board a train, and ride it all the way down to El Paso. He can be in Monterrey in less than a week. Incredible. The hot money he's dumping down there must be flooding the whole state of Nuevo León."

The outside door opened. Ellie Titus appeared, carrying a tray draped with napkins. Hobie came in behind her, coughing into the back of his hand, carrying a rifle as if it weighed fifteen pounds, noted Doc. Horses rumbled by outside as he closed the door.

"Boys comin' back," said Hobie to Ellie offhandedly.

Good Lord, thought Doc, there were more of them.

She came in smiling, nodding first to Titus, then to him. "Soup's on," she said brightly. "Hungry, dear?"

"Please don't call me 'dear.' "

"Oh. Sorry." She sighed. "You *are* taking this to heart, aren't you?"

Titus turned his back on her as she entered the cell area. Hobie came forward with the key, unlocking the door. She came in, and he closed and locked it behind her. She nodded him back out into the office. He stood against the front door, legs spread apart, his rifle at parade rest. He looked ridiculous. Doc's glance strayed to Ellie as she removed the napkins, revealing bread, cheese, a soup of some sort, an opened tin of sardines, and a pot of coffee. She wasn't taunting her husband, calling him 'dear,' he decided, she was only being solicitous. She was uncommonly beautiful, every feature perfect, her eyes, her extraordinary mouth . . . Small wonder Titus was crazy about her.

But, thought Doc, she was just as uncommonly stupid, encumbered with a brain the size of a chickpea. No woman with anything like intelligence would have allowed herself to be drawn into a marriage so obviously doomed from the onset. Raider would have described Ellie Titus perfectly, if coarsely. What brains she had were between her legs. Still, she had interceded on their behalf, had saved their lives for the moment.

"Mrs. Titus . . ."

"Mr. Weatherbee? Do you like cheddar cheese?"

"Yes, thank you, this is very kind."

"I promise you'll both be fed, on time and decently. As long as I'm around."

"And how long will that be?"

"What?"

"When are you and Hungerford leaving again?" asked Titus pointedly.

"Not for a while, Erland. Why?"

"Because as soon as you do, his men will kill us."

"Oh, no. You're wrong, dear."

"Please don't call me 'dear'!"

"I'm sorry, I did it again, didn't I? Tsk, tsk, force of habit."

Titus flinched perceptibly, as if she had stuck him with a pin.

"Your husband's right, they'll kill us. They have to, they have to protect themselves."

"Stuff! Oh, it's true, Benjie does have to protect himself, but only a few weeks longer. Then we'll all be leaving."

"Where to?" asked Doc, fishing.

"Down to . . ." She caught herself. "Oh my, aren't you the clever one? But you're wrong, no one's going to harm either of you, though I can't promise about the boy. Benjie's terribly angry over his getting away."

She poured them coffee. Doc nodded thanks and started to drink his, then paused.

"Did you prepare all this yourself?" he asked.

"Yes."

"Even the coffee?"

"Everything. In the kitchen in the back of the general store, why?"

"While you were fixing it or afterwards, did you by chance leave the room?"

"No."

"Was anybody with you?"

"Hobie came in when I called to tell him it was ready."

"Not Wallace?"

"No."

Titus forced a smile. "Mr. Weatherbee is worried we might be getting a little arsenic with our supper."

"Oh no, Wally wasn't anywhere near." She paused and clucked. "He is such a vicious little man. Benjie's forever getting him out of trouble. He'll be the death of him. You've no idea."

"We've a good idea," said Titus. "He's killed half of Blacktower."

"Not half. Only twenty or thirty people."

"You make it sound like cats. You amaze me. Doesn't it trouble your conscience to be running with thieves and killers?"

"I haven't killed anyone. I haven't stolen anything."

"Not even my key to the bank?"

"Oh, that. I didn't steal it, I borrowed it. Just long enough to make a copy."

"Mrs. Titus, whether you believe it or not, Erland's quite right. Sooner or later, these people are going to have to kill us, regardless of what Hungerford has told you. Even if they leave, they've got to cover their tracks."

She looked from one to the other. "Benjie gave me his solemn word . . ."

"It doesn't matter what he gave you!" snapped Titus

irritably. "He's got to kill us, don't you understand? God in Heaven, must you be so insufferably dense!"

"You're being rude, Erland. And in front of a stranger." She sniffled. "Here I slave over a hot stove, I bring you the neatest, nicest, most delicious dinner, hot coffee and everything, and you bawl me out. You are the limit!"

"I'm sorry, dear, really. I apologize. I'm just . . . a trifle nervous."

"I should say you are. Did you remember to bring your Dr. Mumm's? It's his nerve medicine, she explained to Doe. He's supposed to take two teaspoonfuls a day, every day. Did you bring it, Erland?"

"Damn it no! El, for God's sakes! That's the last thing I thought about."

"Tsk, tsk, tsk. Well, I'll look around the store. Maybe I can find something. Eat up, both of you, don't worry about arsenic. Hobie'll pick up your things when you're done. I have to get back now. Benjie's waiting. Hobie . . ."

He came and let her out.

"Good-bye for now. Sleep well, dear . . . Erland. I'll be back in the morning with your breakfast. Good night, Mr. Weatherbee. And don't worry, everything's going to be all right. You'll see."

CHAPTER FOURTEEN

Raider pulled his horse up short, muttering. "This is no good," he murmured, squeezing his stomach with his free hand and spitting.

"What is it now?" asked Algernon impatiently. "Your stomach acting up again? Sending up signals to your brain?"

"Just the reverse. Heading for Sowville's all wrong, I tell you. Huggens is dead right. A man on the run doesn't move on to the next town. That's the last place he heads for. What he does is cut for the hills. That's where the saying comes from, and it's true. Besides, you heard Huggens, saying how he's sending his wanted dodgers up and down the line. By the time we get there, Sowville'll be plastered with 'em."

"We've searched the plains, Raider. We found nothing but empty shacks and cold fires."

"I said head for the hills." He pointed northwest. "If he isn't long gone, that's where he's at. Got to be. If we don't find him there . . ."

"What then, give up?"

"Let's go."

He reined his horse right and galloped off. They rode at a brisk pace for upwards of an hour, bringing the bluffs of the Llano Estacado into view; behind them, the dim outline of the San Miguel Mountains. It was growing dark. Neither moon nor stars appeared; the sky became swollen with clouds. A distant coyote howled eerily, then was silent. On they rode, their horses beginning to lather. Again Raider pulled up. He sat perfectly still.

"What is it?" asked Algernon.

"Sssssh." He dismounted, handing his reins to the Englishman. "Give me your handkerchief."

"Raider, you're not wiping down your horse with . . ."

"Course I'm not, damn it. Give it to me!"

He practically snatched the silk handkerchief from Algernon's grasp. Kneeling, he spread it on the ground, pulling the corners out taut and leaning over, placed his right ear hard against it.

"What . . .?"

"Sssssh." He listened, straightened, and nodded knowingly. "Horses, and shooting dead ahead." Snatching up the handkerchief, he tossed it to Algernon, mounted up, and spurred off.

"I didn't hear a bloody thing."

"You got to listen through the handkerchief. It's got to be silk."

"Poppycock!"

"The hell it is. It works. The old plainsmen call it long-earring. The handkerchief has to be silk. It magnifies sound. I tell you I heard horses and shots coming from dead ahead."

He picked up the pace; Algernon did his best to stay abreast of him. Now the horses were less than one hundred fifty yards ahead of them. A man came stumbling toward them. Raider reined up hard, and his mount lifted up on its hind legs, whinnying loudly, pawing the air. The man fell on his face and lay still. Raider was down beside him. Algernon started to dismount.

"Stay put!" Raider tossed him his Winchester. "Keep your eyes skinned up ahead. Whoever's after this fellow won't be wanting witnesses." He cocked one ear. The riders ahead of them were turning about. Their hoofbeats grew fainter; the sound soon vanished altogether. Raider bent low and slowly, carefully, turned the man over.

"He's been hit in at least four or five places. He's bleeding like a pig. Who did this, kid?"

Algernon had dismounted and was standing beside Raider. "Son . . ." he began.

The boy's lips parted, closed, and parted. "Doc . . ."

"We'll get you a doctor," said Raider. "Don't worry."

He tried to add something, but could not; the effort was too much for him. His eyes closed, his face fell to one side.

"He's dead," said Algernon.

Raider pressed his ear against his chest. "His heart's still beating, just barely. We got to get him back to town."

"It must be twenty miles."

"I don't care if it's fifty. Help me get him up in front of my tree. We've got to take him in, got to chance it. We leave him be, big and strong as he is, he'll be dead in an hour."

He pulled off his shirt, tearing the sleeves free, and began binding up the boy's wounds.

They had to carry him up twenty-two steps to Dr. Wesley Reichert's office over the Wells Fargo & Company freight office. By his own admission, Reichert was Blacktower's "oldest and only licensed practitioner of medicine and surgery." What he was doing in his rank-smelling little office at twenty minutes past ten at night, Raider couldn't imagine. But he was too grateful and they were too preoccupied with the business at hand to inquire. The place was a bastion of disorder, a jumble of equipment, furniture, and medicines in every conceivable shape and size bottle, occupying virtually every available inch of space. The doctor was a wizened leprechaun, lacking only the picture-book goblin getup, with a horseshoe of fluffy, cottonlike hair girdling his pate, gold-filled spectacles, all bones and skin, energy, caustic tongue, and business.

"Some gang of renegades been using him for target practice, have they? Poor bastard's got more holes in him than a milk skimmer. He must have the constitution of an ox." He adjusted his glasses, taking a closer look at his patient's face. "By Tubal, I know this boy. He's the young fellow who's been sparking Florry-Mae Purinton, the little girl who works over at Poindexter's."

Eustace groaned and stirred.

"Look at him, he's trying to prove he's still alive. Take

it easy, son. We'll get these rags off you and see if we can haul out some of that lead. Hand me that solution of carbolic acid, the brown stuff.'' Reichert indicated a bottle to Raider. ''One of you get over to Addison Spaulding's rooming house, get Florry-Mae, and bring her here.''

''What earthly good will that do?'' asked Algernon.

''I don't know, but it won't do any harm.'' Reichert paused, jerking his head back like an alerted hen. He peered over the tops of his glasses at Algernon. ''You're British.''

''To the core.''

''I thought so. Why is it you people always have to ask questions before you do anything? Just go get her. Down the corner to Weir's Clothing Store, around it, second house on your right, the one with the caved-in stoop. We'll see if we can keep him alive until she gets here.''

Algernon left. Raider positioned himself beside Reichert.

''Are you going to be able to take this as well as he's going to have to?'' asked the doctor, grinning. ''Or do you plan to go queasy on me?''

''I don't have the world's greatest gut, but I've seen my share of bullet holes and blood. Just get to work on him and tell me what to do as you go along.''

Reichert began administering chloroform. ''You can help, all right. Keep that cloth in place over his nose and mouth. His breathing's shallow. If it gets any shallower, lift it off. I just want him in a deep enough sleep so's he won't jump off the table when I start digging.'' He selected a probe from among a number laid out on a cloth.

''You say you found him about twenty miles out of town?''

''On the way to the Buttes, crawling on his belly.''

''I'm not surprised. This much lead must get a little heavy to lug. Ha ha. Amazing, you rode him all the way in in this condition. He *is* an ox. What were you two doing out there?''

Raider got out the wanted poster. ''Looking for this bastard.''

''At night?''

"We've been out most of the day. We figured to stay out and bedroll it."

"What'd he do, shoot somebody? He's not the one who killed Reverend Culpepper, is he?"

"He poisoned twenty-one people."

Reichert paused in his probing. "So that's the son of a bitch. I'd like to have him here. I had to dose half the town with charcoal and tea to wash out their guts, though I doubt if any of them swallowed any arsenic. A pinch is enough to kill you. He picked the lock on Poindexter's supply room door, right?"

"And spiked a barrel of rotgut."

"Nasty-looking bastard, isn't he?" He resumed working. "Come out of there, you bugger. How come you two are doing the chasing? What's the matter with the marshal?"

"He's been looking."

"Huggens is a good soul. Conscientious, I suppose, but he sure doesn't have much follow-through. Never did find who murdered Culpepper. I doubt he'll find your friend there without help. Ah, here comes number one." He held up the slug and dropped it clinking into a basin.

Raider considered Reichert's comments on Marshal Huggens. The doctor wasn't wrong. Huggens had impressed him all along as one who preferred to go through the motions. He had the barrel, the suspect's picture, all sorts of theories and conjectures, but he didn't have the man, or any promise of him. Raider couldn't help thinking about some of the lawmen he'd run into over the years, the outstanding ones, men who would ride a mount into the ground and themselves all but into the grave to catch their quarry, the tenacious types who never gave up on a case, regardless of how long it took to wrap it up. Men who thought more of the responsibility of the office than the star that went with it.

Still, he couldn't fault Huggens on this one. He had tried to find Jasper Wilke, or whatever his real name was. He was still trying; he didn't have the resources or the manpower to drop everything else and track him to Kingdom Come.

Algernon returned.

"Not home?" asked Reichert, without looking up from his probing.

"Out with friends. I left word."

Eustace stirred.

"He's starting to come out of it. Give him a couple more drops of chloroform. I've got three out and two to go. Where in Tubel is all this blood coming from? He must hold six gallons!"

"Did you find out who he is and what he was doing out in that godforsaken spot?" Algernon asked Raider.

"Not exactly. We haven't exactly been chinning like two old pals since you left."

Algernon made his characteristic something-doesn't-smell-all-that-good face and, without a word, strode to the patient's side, slipped his hand under his butt, and brought out his billfold. Reichert snickered, again without looking up. Raider said something foul under his breath. Algernon gasped.

"By Jove!"

"What?" asked Raider.

"Look at this card. His name's Eustace Hillbank. He's a Pinkerton operative!"

"Give me that." Raider snatched the I.D. card from Algernon's hands. Algernon snatched back. Raider twisted about, shouldering him away. "Cut it out, damn it. Let me see here. Jesus, you're right!"

"Who do you suppose his partner is?"

"Could be any one o' fifty guys. An old hand, more'n likely." He studied Eustace's face. Slowly, the unmistakable glint of recognition crept into his eyes. "I know this boy. I've seen him someplace. Where in hell . . .?"

"Chicago?" asked Algernon helpfully.

"No, no, no. Out here in the territories. That face, that hair." He scowled, forcing his way deeper into memory. It was useless. Try as he might, he couldn't place him.

"Think!" snapped Algernon.

"I am, damn it. Don't start up with me."

"Hold it down, you two. Damn, this one's in a foot deep. One of you hold the lamp up. Hang on, son, keep breathing. Only two to go."

CHAPTER FIFTEEN

Erland Titus was becoming more deeply depressed by the hour, noted Doc, studying his cellmate. His wife's visit, her flippant manner, her all too obvious satisfaction with her situation had combined to jolt him into realizing that he didn't have a chance in hell of winning her back. As slender as the thread may have been, to that hope he had been clinging for weeks. Now, with her help, he at last recognized it for what it was, all that it was: delusion.

"You think Eustace got through?" he asked quietly, morosely.

"You've asked me that thirty times," replied Doc. "I keep telling you, your guess is as good as mine."

"You know him better." Titus sighed. "I hate this."

"I'm not exactly enamored of it."

"I don't mean being taken prisoner, I mean Ellie's being involved. It's so degrading. I feel . . . emasculated. I'm a cuckold, a laughingstock to them."

"What do you care what they think? You haven't done anything. You can't control her devil. If she herself can't, how can you expect to? Frankly, I think you've behaved admirably. I think you have mettle and tenacity. You're a man in every sense of the word. You can hold your head up and tell the world, and I'll vouch for it."

"You're not afraid, are you?"

"No? I'm petrified. Who wouldn't be?" The outside door creaked open. "Visitors."

"I hope it's not El again. I can't even stand looking at her."

146

Doc peered out. Three people were coming in. Scofield held his lantern up, revealing Mrs. Titus and Ben Hungerford. They came back to the cells.

"Gentlemen," said Hungerford airily. "How are we doing?"

"Excellently," said Doc. "Although you might send the maid in to change the linen. And, oh yes, the champagne was a trifle bitter."

"I like you, Mr. Pinkerton, you're amusing. I wish I could make *you* laugh. Unfortunately, all I have is bad news."

"Eustace?"

"Dead, I'm afraid." He looked toward Scofield.

"We caught up with him a few miles out on the plains. We threw enough lead into him to sink a cow."

"Congratulations, you bastard!"

"Who you calling . . . ?"

Scofield lunged forward; Hungerford stayed him with his forearm.

"Easy, Mahlon. It was unavoidable, friend. You understand. I don't have to draw pictures, do I?"

"Did your cretins at least have the decency to bury him?"

Scofield sniffed and yawned. "Didn't have time. Had to get back. The wind'll cover him up."

"Were you good friends?" asked Mrs. Titus solicitously, wide-eyeing Doc.

The question was stupid, uncalled for, undeserving of response, but he responded anyway.

"He was my son."

She gasped.

"He doesn't mean that literally, sweetheart," interposed Hungerford.

"I *am* sorry," she said.

"I'm sure you are." Doc stared at her. "For everything. What you've done to your husband, the fact that you'll be an accomplice to his murder, to mine."

Hungerford beamed expansively. "That is utter nonsense,

friend. We have no plans to kill either of you. Unless, of course, you also try to escape.''

"See, Erland," piped his wife. "I told you not to worry."

"El, shut up!''

Hungerford's smile darkened. "Here now, is that any way to talk to your wife? Mister, she saved your bacon.''

"He loves to be nasty to me, rude. Erland, I've brought you some pills for your nerves." She held up a small bottle. "Sears, Roebuck Celery Malt Compound. Take it, dear.''

"Damn it, El!''

"I mean *Erland*.'' She glanced uneasily at Hungerford. "He doesn't like me to call him 'dear' anymore.''

Titus refused to take the bottle from her. Doc accepted it for him.

"You don't have a deck of cards, do you?'' he asked Hungerford.

"I'm sure we can scare some up.''

"I'd appreciate it. Can I ask you a question?'' He got a soft scowl of permission. "Mr. Titus and I have a little wager going. He says your Mexico outlet is in Monterrey. I'm guessing Reynosa.''

"You lose.''

"How big is your take so far?''

"Big.''

"A million?''

Again Hungerford smiled. "You'll know soon enough. You two are going to start work in the bank first thing in the morning. I can use your expertise, Erland, and I'm sure you, Mr. Pinkerton, are well past counting on your fingers. Good night for now. Mahlon will bring you that deck of cards and a fruit crate you can use for a table.''

"And blankets," said Mrs. Titus.

"Of course. Only no maid and no champagne." Hungerford snickered.

"Good night, Mr. Weatherbee," she said gaily. "Good night, Erland. Don't forget to take your medicine. Mr.

Weatherbee, you see that he does. I do so worry about him.''

Again Hungerford laughed, but, Doc noted, his eyes had a predatory look in them. He wanted them dead and out of his way as soon as possible. No mistake. Doc sighed silently. Neither of them would ever see the inside of his bank again.

Eustace lay on the table unconscious, his breath coming lightly, his massive chest, bound laterally with clean gauze, rising and falling almost indiscernibly. Alongside his left forearm was the basin; in it the five slugs. Reichert rolled down his sleeves, rebuttoned his vest, went about plowing through his desk, slamming drawers, found a stogie and touched a kitchen match to it, producing an immense cloud of foul-smelling blue smoke.

"Is he going to make it, Doc?" asked Raider worriedly.

"I think so, if he stays put. Look at his face, pale as new snow. If he loses one more ounce of blood, he'll be tapped out."

He had taken an hour and a half by the little Saxon octagon clock on the wall over his desk to extract the slugs and bandage his patient. It was now close to midnight. They heard footsteps outside.

"Either of you like stogies?" asked Reichert. "Pollock's Crown. Fourteen bucks a thousand."

They shook their heads, Raider silently, wistfully wishing that Reichert didn't like stogies. The smoke was beginning to make him sick to his stomach, bringing back thoughts of Doc Weatherbee and his Old Virginia cheroots.

Florry-Mae came pounding in, all out of breath. She wore a plain double-wool shawl over a magenta dress dotted with sequins. In her hair was a matching magenta ostrich feather that looked to Raider as if it had been pulled through a keyhole, so frazzled was it.

"*Eustace!*"

She would have flung herself across his chest if Raider hadn't intervened, catching her before she got to the table and swinging her about.

"Easy, easy, he's hurting bad."

"Oh, Eustace, Eustace!" She broke free and ran to him, covering his head with kisses, combing his hair with her fingers. "Sweety lumps."

"Sweety lumps?" Reichert gaped foolishly, his stogie threatening to drop from his mouth.

"Will he live?" she asked, goggle-eyeing him worriedly.

"He may if you keep your paws off him and your voice down so he can get some sleep."

"How did it happen?"

Reichert turned to Raider.

"Out on the plains."

"He'd evidently been captured by someone and got away," said Algernon. "He didn't have a horse, no firearms."

"Captured by who? Not that banker . . .?"

"What banker?" asked Raider.

"The one from down south, Baptist Wells. I can't remember his name."

Algernon shook his head. "We have no idea who's responsible."

"Where's Doc?"

"Eh?" asked Reichert, looking up. He had been smoking contentedly, wholly absorved in his Pollack's Crown, only half listening to the conversation.

"Doc Weatherbee."

Raider's jaw dropped. His eyes met Algernon's. He seized Florry-Mae, locking her arms tightly to her sides. "Doc Weatherbee? Eustace's partner?"

"Yes."

"What were they doing out there?"

"Looking for the banker."

"What's his name? Try and remember."

"I'm trying, I can't."

Eustace stirred. Raider turned to him.

"He's waking up. Good. We got to question him, Doc."

"Not a chance."

"It's a matter of life and death."

"You bet it is, his and his. This boy's going to sleep all

day and all tomorrow night, if he can. He's my patient, and doctor knows best. Now, I want all three of you out.'' He nodded toward a cot in the corner. ''I'm tired, I'm going to bed.''

''One question, that's all,'' persisted Raider. ''Just one, please.''

''Not even half a one.'' Reichert raised his arms, ushering them toward the door.

''Okay, okay, goddamn it, be pig-headed!''

''That's me all over.''

''Only if he does wake up, you ask him. We want to know where exactly Weatherbee is.''

''I'd better write it down, I got a lot on my mind lately.'' He began redistributing the clutter on his desk, searching for a pencil. Algernon got out his black book and scribbled in it, ripping out the page.

''Heatherbee?'' asked Reichert blankly, reading it.

''That's a 'W.' Weatherbee.''

''We'll be back,'' said Raider. ''Take good care o' that boy.''

Reichert grunted and waved them out the door with both hands.

They stood at the top of the steps in the darkness, Florry-Mae sniffling into a hanky, Raider trying his utmost to comfort her, his right arm set charily around her shoulders.

''He was coming from the Buttes,'' he said. ''Were they heading for there? Did he happen to mention any particular place he and Doc would be going to look for this banker?''

''All over, riding a big circle around Blacktower.''

''That sounds familiar,'' said Algernon dryly.

''We'll take you on back to your place,'' said Raider, ignoring him.

They walked slowly up the street. Blacktower was asleep, few lights in windows, Poindexter's still shuttered. Pausing at the corner, they looked back. Dr. Reichert's office was now in darkness. They turned the corner, stopping in front of the gate to Addison Spaulding's rooming house.

Raider got out the wanted dodger, holding it up to the feeble light emanating from the parlor windows.

"You recognize this fellow?"

"I've seen him. He passed Eustace, me, and Doc on the street one evening. He poisoned the whiskey at Poindexter's, didn't he?"

"That's what he's wanted for," said Algernon. "We want him for poisoning cattle. You don't, by chance, know his name?"

"Never heard it. We never spoke." She paused, knitting her brow in thought.

"What?" asked Raider.

"Come to think of it, Eustace mentioned just the other day that Doc was standing at the bar in Poindexter's when that fellow got thrown out for causing a to-do."

"Then Doc's seen more of him than either you or Eustace." She nodded. "Does this picture look like him?"

"Exactly like him, big hat and all. Except it doesn't show his limp, of course."

Algernon beamed. "That settles it. He has to be our man."

"I thought we'd decided that a long time ago." Raider raised his hat. "Good night, Miss Purinton. Thanks for all your help. Don't worry about Eustace, he's tough as they come. He'll be up and around before you know it."

"He will. My sweety lumps," she added dreamily. She nodded to each of them in turn and went inside.

"What now?" asked Algernon. "What am I saying?" He stifled a yawn. "I beg your pardon. Let's go to bed, shall we, old boy?"

"I'd rather we go back out. We can sleep out there as easy as we can here."

"Not nearly as easy, easily. Dear me, I'm bloody well beginning to talk like you. Let's be practical. Let's wait until Eustace comes around. He'll be able to give us precise directions."

"Sure. *When* he comes around. Which might not be for three days. In the meantime, Doc's out there maybe chained up, maybe tortured, even dying. Who knows what the hell's going on. I say we head back out pronto.''

"You head back out prrrrr-onto. I'm going to bed, thank you.''

So saying, he turned on his heel and strode away in the direction of the Hotel Blodgett.

"Go ahead and go screw yourself, while you're at it, Mr. hard-boiled hat and funny fat pants!''

And abruptly realizing that he had no shirt on, Raider swore in disgust and followed him.

CHAPTER SIXTEEN

Raider and Algernon returned to Dr. Reichert's office a few minutes after nine the next morning. Florry-Mae was already there. The doctor was hard at work on his third stogie of the day, bluing the air in the little office. The stench assailed Raider's nostrils and turned his breakfast in his stomach slightly. Reichert looked as if he'd slept in his clothes, and his fringe of long white hair suggested that he had been fanning it vigorously, causing it to stand straight out from his scalp. Eustace slept on, an angelic smile bowing his thick lips. Raider sighed in relief at the sight of him; at least he'd gotten through the night. He looked better. His color was beginning to come back, and his breathing appeared normal.

"When's he going to wake up, Doc?" Raider asked, ignoring the passing thought that hinted at the stupidity of the question.

"Why don't you ask me how long before the roof caves in?" growled Reichert. "You two come in here with your dumb questions. Florry-Mae brings him beef broth."

She nodded affirmation. A large pot sat on the squat, chubby Globe Lighthouse stove in the corner. Alongside the pot a tea kettle whistled softly.

"If it's all the same to you, I want to find my sidekick before whoever's got him finishes him off," said Raider icily. "The way they tried to finish Eustace. I can understand your wanting to protect him. You might try understanding the other side o' the dollar."

Reichert glared balefully. "I flatter myself that I do. What you fail to appreciate is that my turning you loose on

154

Eustace might upset him in his present delicate condition. Get him all hot and bothered, and completely reverse his recovery. He's just beginning to come back. It's not just his wounds, it's the shock to his system. I'm not about to risk losing him just so you can find out what's going on with somebody who may very well be dead and gone already. Is that clear?''

Algernon stepped in front of Raider. "Perfectly clear, Doctor. You must excuse my associate. He's something less than diplomatic by nature, and he has at best a tenuous hold on his patience.''

"Will you shut up!'' said Raider.

"*You* shut up,'' rasped Reichert. "Or get your ass out and stay out.'' He cleared his throat. "Pardon my French, Florry-Mae.''

Eustace stirred, moaning softly and licking his lips.

"He's waking up,'' said Raider, starting toward the table.

Reichert scowled. "Stay where you are.''

"He's sweating something awful,'' said Florry-Mae.

"His fever's up. You've got to expect that. Get a cloth over there, fold it, dip it in the bucket, wring it out, and lay it across his forehead. Good girl.''

"Doc,'' murmured Eustace.

"I'm here, son,'' said Reichert.

"Weatherbee.''

"Please, Doctor,'' entreated Raider. "One question, just one.''

Reichert started to object, then abruptly changed his mind. "One, then the two of you get out.''

Raider nodded. "Deal.''

He leaned over the table. "Eustace, I'm Raider, Doc Weatherbee's old sidekick. Eustace, where is he? Where's Doc?''

Eustace's eyes opened. "Everything's foggy. . . . Oooooh.''

"Take it easy,'' said Raider.

Florry-Mae laid the cloth across his forehead.

"Where've they got Doc?'' repeated Raider.

"Foothill trail. Up 'bout a mile.'' He paused and licked his lips. "Thirsty.''

Florry-Mae came over with a tumbler of water and wet his lips with it, using a corner of her hanky.

"Foothill trail, up about a mile,'' said Raider.

"To . . . big rock . . . big as a house . . . round it . . . stick to trail . . . mile and a half . . . Blacktower.''

Raider frowned in puzzlement.

"He means Old Blacktower,'' said Reichert. "Old silver town. Only nobody ever found any silver, so they abandoned it. It's been a ghost town for years.''

"Sounds like somebody's moved in,'' said Raider. "Eustace . . .''

"That's enough,'' said Reichert sternly, shoving his arm in front of Raider, easing him back from the table. "You've had your question, you got your answer. Now get out.''

Eustace's eyes closed, his head lolling to one side. Florry-Mae started.

"He's all right, he's all right,'' said Reichert.

"Thank you, Doctor,'' said Algernon.

"Yeah, yeah.''

They stood outside on the little balcony overlooking an alley littered with rubbish and sending up the stink of rotten meat. Two cats were busy foraging.

"Let's get over to Huggens's office,'' said Raider. "We're going to need help on this one.''

"A ghost town. Amazing. I would think that would be the first place Huggens would search for Jasper Wilke.''

"Maybe he did. Maybe there was nobody out there then.''

Algernon shook his head. "He didn't, old fellow. Those foothills are thirty or forty miles from here. He never went past the five-mile mark. He told us that early on, don't you recall?''

"Who cares? What are we standing here jawing about it for? Come on.''

Huggens was not in his office. One of his deputies was. He was past sixty, with a salt and pepper beard, a florid complexion, and a single brown and crooked tooth surviving in his lower gum that threatened to pierce his upper lip when he spoke.

"Marshal ain't here."

"We can see that," grumbled Raider. "Where . . .?"

"Him and the rest o' the boys went down to Elkins on the train last night. Big goings-on. Don't know exactly what. Nobody told me. Nobody tells me nothing. They won't be back for a day or two, though. I know that much. Left me to hold the fort."

"Jesus Christ!" said Raider.

"Did you want Virgil for something?"

"Yeah, we was hoping to get up a hand o' stud."

The man shook his head. "Virgil don't play poker no more. His missus put the kibosh on it. He once lost a whole month's pay."

Raider cut him off, slamming the door behind them.

"Goddamn it to hell!" he bellowed outside. "If this doesn't beat all!"

Florry-Mae was coming toward them all smiles, waving gaily.

"Eustace is awake. He wants to sit up, but Doc won't let him."

"Good for him," said Algernon.

Raider grunted. "That boy's tougher than a Texas toad. He must eat iron and spit out nails."

"You fellows want to come back and ask him more questions? Doc says it's okay to. He's going to be all right, he is!" She squealed, flung out her arms, and spun around. "My sweety lumps, my sweety lumps!"

Raider and Algernon exchanged glances.

"We don't need to ask him anything else right now," said Raider. "Just tell him we're heading out to get Doc."

"That is, we would like to head out," said Algernon. "We were hoping to enlist the help of Marshal Huggens and his men, but they're evidently not available. They've left town."

"You want help? I can get you all you need. Best shooting eyes in Blacktower, you bet."

Raider brightened. "Can you round up, say, ten or a dozen?"

"Easy as pie."

"Then get at it. We'll head on out. One of us'll stick by the big rock on the foothills trail Eustace spoke of and meet 'em. Make it fast, little girl, there's a good man out there we got to save."

"There's a good man in here *I* got to save. Me and Eustace are getting hitched. I'm on my way to the blacksmith's shop right now. Sumner Tibbs, the smith, is a justice o' the peace. We're going to be married up in Doc's office. You're invited, if you can spare ten minutes. Soon as we say 'I do,' I'll go and get your help for you, but first things first!"

So saying, she whirled about and walked off humming happily to herself.

CHAPTER SEVENTEEN

Doc was wrong; he and Titus made it through the night, through breakfast prepared by Titus's doting ex-wife, and to work at the bank. Hungerford set them to counting packets of bills and checking down interminably long lists of serial numbers. The work was boring but, Doc conceded to himself, better bored than buried. Rafe and Wallace also worked in the bank. That is, Rafe worked, swamping out the place and tidying up the contents of the vault; Wallace held down a tall stool, his rifle in his lap, picking at his nose and tossing snide remarks at the two prisoners. He wore a piece of court plaster on his chin where Scofield had hit him. Occasionally Rafe would tell him to lay off needling, but with nothing like Scofield's insistence and without any threat to make him if he didn't.

He was a tedious little man, reflected Doc, glancing up from his work and looking at him out of the corner of his eye every so often. He was preoccupied completely with bullying, sounding off in a vain effort to make himself appear important, in charge. A silly little man.

"I bet you never seen so much money, Mr. Banker. Bet you never dreamed what was gonna happen to your bank when we stole it. Nobody ever done that before, I bet. Man, that vault door's heavier than a Conestoga wagon. Took twelve of us to lift it. Why the hell do they make 'em so big and heavy, do you think? Don't seem to me it has to be *that* big. Why is that, do you suppose?"

"To give you a hernia to remember the experience by," murmured Doc.

"Oh hey, that's funny. Did you hear what he said,

Rafe? He said they make 'em so big and heavy to give you
a hernia to remember lifting it by.''

"I heard, Wallace. Can you stop talking awhile? My
ears is starting to ring.''

"You go to hell. What you looking at, Mr. Banker?
Them horses at the hitch rack 'cross the way? Hey, what if
Rafe stayed inside the vault stacking things an' I just
dozed off here on this stool. You two could sneak out the
door, skedaddle on over there, grab yourselves a couple
mounts, and take off, right? You'd like to do that, wouldn't
you?''

Doc had crossed that bridge on their way to the bank
earlier. And dismissed the thought. It posed the perfect
solution to Hungerford's little problem. Justifiable homicide:
shot while trying to escape. Mrs. Titus wouldn't like it, but
she'd undoubtedly buy it. Lord, but she was dense, and
about as sensitive as a rampaging longhorn. Insisting Erland
take his nerve medicine, as if he was concerned over his
nerves at this stage. If he somehow survived, he'd never
need to dose his nerves again.

If he survived; neither of them had a chance in hell of
surviving!

"Can we go down this third column again?" Titus
asked, breaking into his thoughts. Doc nodded, half laughing quietly. "What's funny?"

"You. You're taking this job seriously.''

"I guess I am. Force of habit. When I see figures that
don't jibe I get positively antsy. They simply have to come
out right.''

"You two cut out talking so much," said Wallace,
waving the rifle.

"We're trying to straighten something out," averred
Titus.

"Do it without talking.''

Wallace was getting fidgety. He kept shifting his weapon
from one hand to the other, tapping one foot against the
leg of the stool, unable to reach the floor, attacking his
nose with his index finger disgustingly.

"Hey, Rafe," he said at length. "Keep an eye on these

two. I'm going over to the store an' get me a cup o' coffee.''

"I'm busy, can't you see? I can't keep guard and work, too. Just hold on a few minutes.''

"Like hell. I want coffee, damn it. Go get us both some, can't you? Be a sport.''

"Later, I'm busy.''

"Prick.''

"Don't start calling names, Wallace. I don't have to take your shit.''

"I just want some damn coffee.''

"So send one of 'em on over.''

"Hey, that's a good idee. Never thought o' that. You, Pink, go get me an' Rafe some coffee.''

"Get it yourself.''

Wallace stood up, gripping the rifle, glaring. "Get movin' afore I kick your ass out the door.''

"I'll get it,'' said Titus resignedly.

"I don't want you, I want him. You, Pink, move!''

"Okay.''

Doc's change of mind momentarily startled Wallace. He reacted nonplussed, then motioned him out the door. Mrs. Titus was in the rear room of the general store. A pot of coffee stood on the stove, vapor issuing from its spout.

"Good morning again, Mr. Weatherbee,'' she said brightly. "How's work going?''

"Just fine.''

"It's nice to see you. Guess what.''

"I can't imagine.''

"I found some Dr. Mumm's, Erland's nerve medicine. I'll give you a teaspoon and you take it back to him.''

He also got four tin cups. She gave him a basket, and he filled it with the pot, the cups, the medicine, and a spoon. The coffee was piping hot. A crazy, wild, simple, but undeniably risky plan hatched in the back of his mind. The pot was about half full. He'd get Wallace to check and see if there was enough coffee and when he looked, toss it in his face, grab the rifle, and wallop Rafe.

Wallace was still perched on the stool when he got

back, but no longer holding the rifle. Rafe had it behind a
cash window, busy polishing the stock with a piece of
lamb's wool. Momentarily blinding Wallace by tossing
coffee in his face would accomplish nothing, apart from
alerting Rafe, prompting him to let go with a couple shots.
At ten feet he could hardly miss.

"Let's have it," snapped Wallace. "Over here, let's
have a look."

Doc opened the top for him and he bent over it. Doc
was sorely tempted, but managed to quell the urge.

"Is it hot?" Wallace asked.

"Stick your finger in and see."

"Set it on the table, wise guy. Pour us out some."

"Your wife gave me some Dr. Mumm's," said Doc to
Titus.

"How thoughtful of her," rejoined the banker without
looking up from his figuring.

Raider waited impatiently by the enormous rock above
where the trail turned sharply right then left to head farther
up into the hills. Presently, after what seemed eons, he
spotted dust rising in the distance; under it was a wagon
being drawn by what appeared to be four mules. His heart
beat faster.

"Good girl."

Closer and closer came the wagon. His heart sank slightly.
Something was wrong. None of the men seated facing
each other were wearing hats. The truth dawned on him
like a small bolt of lightning striking the nape of his neck.
None of the men were men. The wagon was now less than
a half-mile distant. It started up the narrow trail, then
stopped. The occupants piled out, wielding assorted rifles.
They wore gowns and gloves and feathers in their hair. It
was Sunday-go-to-meeting for the Ladies Aid Society,
reflected Raider discouragedly, chagrin piling up in his
stomach like an undigested meal. Goddamn Florry-Mae!

They came up the trail Indian file, one hand holding up
a skirt, the other holding an ancient Sharps, a Winchester,
a breech-loading Henry. Florry-Mae led the way; there

were eleven of them in all. The best shooting eyes in Blacktower you bet wore mascara. Eleven whores from Poindexter's.

"Goddamn it to hell! Florry-Mae, what in red hell is all this? You said you'd get—"

"A flock o' good shots. Here they are. This is Zora, Emily June, Priscilla. That's Jade. Her real name's Jane, but she goes by Jade. Come on, girls, shake a leg. Meet Mr. Raider." She introduced everybody in turn. "Now, tell us what we got to do. Oh, by the way, Eustace sends his best and says not to worry about him." She displayed a wedding ring on her finger. "This was my maw's. I'll be getting my very own for-real ring when Eustace is up and about. What do you want us to do? Name it."

"Would you just go back down the hill, get into your wagon, and head on back to town? There's liable to be some shooting fairly soon, and I wouldn't want any o' you to get hurt."

Florry-Mae patted him on the lapel. She addressed him like a doting mother explaining to her small son.

"None of us are planning to get hurt. We all know how to shoot. We're not going to get all panicky on you when the lead starts flying. Trust me, Raider, I know every one o' these girls, and there isn't one who can't knock the head off a crow on the wing at fifty yards. Isn't that so, girls?"

All nodded. He couldn't fail to notice that they looked positively eager to get started.

"Jesus Christ, I don't believe this. You don't understand, Florry-Mae. There's at least a dozen of 'em up there, armed to the teeth. They got to be rousted out. We got to clean out the entire nest before they take it into their heads to shoot Doc and that banker. Providing, that is, they're even still alive. This is going to be a damn bloodbath. No prisoners, just shoot first and count the dead after the smoke clears. You can't—"

"Can't your bellrope, mister! We don't need any whining, puling, and mewling from you. We don't need speeches or arguing. All we want is what we came for: action. So step aside. Stay back here and cool your heels. We'll take over and flush them outta there, every man jack. Outta the way!''

"Okay, okay, okay! Damn it all, you don't give a fella much choice, do you?''

"You don't give a girl much credit.''

"I'm sorry.''

"Don't be. Forget it. Let's just get at it.''

Raider was shocked; Algernon was beside himself, aghast.

"What in the name of . . .?''

He seized Raider by the arm and pulled him aside.

"How could you do this?''

"How could I? Where in hell you get off saying that? *I* didn't do nothing. How was I supposed to know she was going to show up with a wagon load o' whores? She said shooting eyes.''

"Yes, yes, I know. I was there, remember?''

"It could be worse. She could have come back with the kindergarten class.''

"Very funny.''

"I don't think it's funny.''

"Anytime you're ready, there,'' called Florry-Mae impatiently. "We'd like to get started. We didn't plan to spend the whole day out here.''

Ellie Titus came into the bank twenty minutes after Doc returned with the coffee. She had changed into a tight-fitting suit and riding boots and carried her crop.

"Hello again, there,'' she said, according her husband a waggle of her fingers. "I came to tell you that Benjie and I are going to be leaving.''

"So soon?'' asked Doc.

"We just found out we have to. A rider came from Trinidad. He . . . Oh, but you don't want to hear about business.''

She crossed to where Titus was standing in his shirt-sleeves stacking ten-dollar bills. She laid a tentative hand on his arm. He pulled away from her.

"Take care of yourself, Erland.''

"By all means. I'll take my Dr. Mumm's, no fatty foods, eight hours sleep every night. El, you are the most exasperating human being on God's green earth. Can't you get it through your thick head, the minute you're out of sight that animal over there will shoot us in cold blood!"

Wallace glared. "Who you calling an animal?"

Rafe laughed. Wallace whirled on him.

"What the hell's so funny?"

"You."

Wallace started to respond. A shot sounded, followed by two more. Within seconds the sound of rapid firing made it impossible to talk. Mrs. Titus cried out in panic and, before any of them could stop her, ran out into the street. Wallace shouted at her, as did Titus, but she stood as if in shock, her hands upraised defensively, her eyes wide and staring around her at the hilltops. A shot caught her squarely in the forehead. The four of them looking on gasped. Slowly she turned toward them, her knees crumpling, the red spot in her forehead pouring forth blood, streaming down to the bridge of her nose, dividing, slipping down both cheeks. She stood momentarily motionless, knees bent, body hunched forward, her mouth opening slowly. Then she fell in a heap.

"Ellie!" screamed Titus, starting for the door. Doc grabbed him around the waist, pulling him back.

"Get down and stay down!"

Wallace and Rafe had both flattened, Rafe searching the hills above the roofs of the buildings across the street, looking for a target. He fired.

"What the hell you shooting at?" yelled Wallace. "I can't see a goddamn thing!"

"Up top, near that big boulder." Again Rafe fired.

"You're just wasting ammunition!" exclaimed Wallace.

"We can't have that," said Doc to Titus. Up on his feet, he brought his heel down sharply on Rafe's neck. A dull crunching sounded between shots. Rafe went limp, the rifle slipping from his grasp.

"You bas—" began Wallace, his face twisted viciously. It was as far as he got. Titus threw himself at him, slamming him hard against the wall, toppling the stool. Wallace cursed and came up swinging, but Titus got hold of the stool and smashed him in the face with the seat. When he took it away, blood spurted from the little man's nose.

"Son of a bitch!" snarled Wallace.

Doc picked him up to a sitting position with one hand and knocked him cold with the other.

"Look around, see if there's something to tie him with," he rasped.

"Ellie, Ellie, Ellie . . ."

Titus stood immobile, seized by shock, his hands creeping upward to cover his face. Tears streamed down his cheeks.

"Erland, for God's sakes, move!"

"Wha . . . oh, yes, something to tie him with." He cast about and found some empty money sacks. Using his penknife, he cut the drawstrings from around their tops and tied them together. Doc, meanwhile, had turned Wallace over on his belly.

"We'll tie him cradle," he said.

"Cradle?"

"Wrists behind his back. Legs up so. Ankles tied to his wrists. I'll hold his legs. Make it fast, he's starting to come out of it."

Titus tied him securely. Doc ripped the court plaster off Wallace's jaw and fixed it over his mouth. Then Doc looked about them. Outside, the shooting had increased in intensity.

"Let's get out of here," shouted Titus above the din.

"Forget it. We wouldn't get ten yards."

"Help me bring her in."

"Leave her alone. Don't set foot out that door, not unless you want your head blown off."

"But . . ."

"She's dead, Erland. Nothing can hurt her now."

"What are we going to do? There's a back door. We could make it to the hole. We could hide there."

"What good'll that do? No. Wait, I've got an idea. Give me a hand."

Together, they dragged Rafe's corpse and Wallace into the vault.

"Can this thing be opened from the inside if it's locked outside?" Doc asked.

"That's impossible. But we could plug the bolt chamber so the bolt can't slide across. If we had something to plug it with."

Doc reentered the vault and pulled the court plaster from Wallace's mouth,

"You son of a bitch!" spat Wallace.

"One more word out of you, little man, and I'll kick your face down your throat!"

"That hurt."

"Shut up."

Titus fixed the court plaster over the end of the bolt chamber, stopping the bolt, preventing it from crossing and entering the jamb chamber. Doc's glance drifted to the spots of Wallace's blood in the corner. Together he and Titus moved a file cabinet over the spots.

"Okay, let's get inside the vault," said Doc.

Florry-Mae had joined Algernon approximately a hundred yards over to the right of Raider. A tall, slender, big-busted blonde lay prone beside him, firing a Winchester.

"I got one and a maybe. He pulled back around the corner of the store, so I can't say for sure," she said in a little-girl voice.

"You handle that thing pretty good," said Raider admiringly.

"For a girl, you mean."

"For anybody."

Two of Florry-Mae's friends had positioned themselves at either end of the arc of attack drawn three quarters of the way around the town. The end positions were under orders to pick off anybody attempting to flee out back in the direction of Tucumcari. Raider put the enemy's strength at fifteen or sixteen guns. From where he lay he could see the dark-haired woman lying in the street in front of the bank. Somebody, he couldn't tell who, had picked her off seconds after she had stepped out the door. She had a very pretty face, beautiful, he thought, even in death. She had not been armed, but whoever had shot her wasn't taking any chances. Florry-Mae and her friends were handling themselves famously under fire. Most of the opposition fire appeared to be coming from the three upstairs windows of the general store. Ricochets sang off the rocks around him, and twice he had had to duck when lead came within inches of his face. One shot hit close, spewing sand into his eyes and mouth, setting him sputtering and cursing.

The battle went on. The girl next to him paused to reload.

"I didn't bring but fifty or so cartridges," she said apologetically. "It was all I had. I didn't think this was going to be a war."

"You'd best space 'em."

"I'll get itchy waiting for a clear shot. I always get itchy waiting. I need something to occupy my mind, you know?" She smiled, winked, and, reaching over, began fumbling at his fly.

"Oh for chrissakes, not now, please?"

"After?"

"Maybe."

"Why maybe, don't you like me?"

"Maybe 'cause maybe one of us'll get our head blown off and won't be around to do anything, won't be fit for nothing but a shovel o' dirt in the face."

"You a worrier?"

"Just thinking practical. This is the hottest and heaviest I've seen in years."

"Me too. Oh, my name's Angela."

"Pleased to meet you. Thanks for coming."

A shout went up. Raider looked to his right. Florry-Mae was still prone, the barrel of her rifle resting across her left forearm. Algernon was up on his knees, his white silk handkerchief tied to the muzzle of his Winchester. He was getting to his feet, calling out.

"I say, down there, cease firing. *Cease Firing!*"

"What the hell?" began Raider.

"Is he nuts?" asked Angela, bewildered.

Algernon was now fully upright, raising his rifle, waving the handkerchief. To Raider's astonishment, the shooting stopped. A voice called up from below.

"What the hell you want, mister?"

Raider gasped. Close by Algernon his little alcohol stove was lit, and on it sat his teapot.

"Thank you," called Algernon. "If I might have everyone's undivided attention. It is now precisely four o'clock. Tea time in my country. I realize I'm not in my country, but that, I'm sure you'll agree, is inconsequential. I would like you all to join me in a cup of tea, but under the circumstances that appears out of the question. Therefore, may I request that all of you on both sides please hold your fire for the next few minutes so that I may enjoy a cup in peace and quiet, following which we can resume the fi—"

A single shot rang out, clipping the brim of his derby, freeing it from his head. It fell to the ground; he too dropped as a barrage came at him.

"I say, of all the bloody cheek! Ill-mannered louts! Philistines! Blackguards!"

Raider groaned, requested heavenly indulgence with his eyes, and resumed firing.

"The man's crazy with the heat," said Angela in wonderment.

"What I wouldn't give for about ten sticks o' Red Star dynamite," said Raider. "I'd wind this thing up in two shakes."

It was giving no sign of ending. The sun was settling into the plain beyond the town, the shadows stretching, joining, and draping the buildings. Lights came on upstairs over the general store and elsewhere, then the lamps and lanterns were moved, removing the glow from the windows. The firing slowed and stopped altogether for a few minutes, before resuming sporadically. Raider bellied backwards and, crouching, ran over to where Algernon and Florry-Mae lay.

"You maniac," he rasped.

"Don't start, Raider. I'm not in the mood to listen. My shoulder aches, I'm tired of lying here like old dog Brutus before the fire, I'm miserable because I've only had two drops of tea. The rest spilled when one of those recreant scoundrels came too close. You don't actually believe your partner is still alive down there, do you?"

"He's alive till we find him dead."

"Why don't you take a stroll down and have a look?"

"Why don't you pull your hard-boiled hat down over your boots!"

"Will you two stop it!" exclaimed Florry-Mae.

"What are we going to do, Raider?" Algernon asked. "We obviously can't attack. We can't get down without exposing ourselves. They're just as obviously prepared to hold out indefinitely. They have food, ammunition in quantity, freedom of movement, and two hostages. We have none of the first, precious little left of the second, and neither of the last two."

"I got a hunch come dark, if it does get dark, no moon, no stars, they'll try to make a break for it. They got to figure us being up here we can easy send back to town for reinforcements."

"I don't see as they have to figure anything like that. They have eyes, they can see we're the only men up here. They must wonder why no men showed up to assist us. They must suspect something's amiss. I don't think they'll try to leave at all. I think they'll send a small detachment up to get us, perhaps try to get round behind us. We certainly can't circle them. We don't have sufficient firepower. Besides, the hills behind the town are much too far back."

"How about if you and me go down there? Florry-Mae here and the rest can cover us."

"Wouldn't that be a trifle rash?"

"It's risky as hell, but it's worth trying. Most of 'em are holed up in the store, at least half. If we get lucky and find Doc and that banker, we'll be four instead of two against—"

"Against at least a dozen. We've been uncommonly

lucky thus far. We've yet to sustain a single casualty. But to blithely, boldly march into the lion's den. Raider, I just don't know.''

''Trust me.''

Florry-Mae laughed. Algernon scowled and muttered something unintelligible.

''What'd you say?''

''I said, Why I left London is more than I can fathom.''

Raider scanned the sky. ''It'll be dark in two hours. Pray for clouds.''

''I feel like an oiled fish in a tin can,'' said Titus drearily. ''The air's getting terribly close.''

Doc opened the vault door and peered out.

''You two are dead, you know that, don't you,'' grumbled Wallace.

''Possibly,'' said Doc. ''But one thing we're not. We're not tied up. Only stupid people let their prisoners turn the tables on them and get themselves in the fix you're in.''

''I was watching all that shooting outside, her getting hit. Ben's going to love that. They was going to get married an' everything,'' he added, glancing at Titus.

The banker scowled witheringly. Doc didn't like the look of him. His eyes were getting a frenzied look, suggesting that he was either on the verge of breaking down, coming apart completely, or going berserk.

''I can speak my mind,'' continued Wallace. ''What's the difference? You're gonna shoot me anyhow.''

''Not right away,'' said Doc. ''We like to save the best till the last. Erland, nobody's fired a shot in at least three minutes.''

''They could start in again anytime.''

''I know. What do you think?''

''About making a run for it? You're the expert in these things. What do you think?''

Doc knit his brow thoughtfully. ''We could try for the grave out back.''

''I wish you'd say hole. I'd feel better about hiding in it.''

"Getting to it shouldn't be hard. The problem is, what do we do once we're there? It's wide open a good two hundred yards to the hills in the back. If anyone was to look around, they could pick us off like gophers."

"I think we ought to stick here. Doc?"

"What?"

"I want to bring El's body inside. Can I?"

"You'd be foolish to try."

"I want to. Will you help me?"

"I've got a better idea. We'll send out a volunteer."

Doc held the rifle fixed squarely on Wallace's chest as Titus untied him.

"Bring her in, Wallace," said Doc.

"She's too heavy for me."

"You can do it. You try anything and you know what'll happen."

"I won't try nothin'. Only it's gettin' real dark. The boys maybe won't know it's me. They may get jumpy and take a shot."

Doc nodded. "That's why you're elected."

Wallace swallowed. He crawled out on hands and knees, the rifle aimed at his backside. He got hold of her under the knees and neck, but he wasn't strong enough to lift her.

"She's too damn heavy," he rasped.

Titus sighed irritably and, before Doc could stop him, was out the door and lending a hand. Two shots started a fusillade. He was hit in the shoulder and leg. Wallace caught one in the hip, falling on his rear, his legs kicking out, spinning him on one haunch.

"I'm hit, I'm hit, I'm hit, I'm hit!"

Titus came staggering in carrying his wife.

"Get back in here, Wallace," blurted Doc. "I'll give you five seconds, then I start shooting!"

"Don't shoot! Don't shoot!"

Wallace came scrambling back inside. Doc footed the door closed, gripping the rifle, peering out from the corner of the window, trying in vain to pinpoint where the shots had come from.

"Are you hit badly?" he asked Titus.

"*I* am!" shrilled Wallace. "I'm bleeding to death. Look at the blood, look!"

"Shut up!" Doc snapped. "Erland . . ."

"Nooooo." Titus's voice trailed off into faintness, but his weakness was not the result of his wounds. His shock was returning. Doc could see his eyes staring sightlessly, his mouth partially open. He had eased his wife's body down. Doc drew the front window shade down to within a half inch of the sill. He lit a lamp, setting it on the file cabinet in the corner.

"Ellie, Ellie." Titus held her close, tears flowing from his eyes, staining his face by the feeble light. "Why did you do it, my darling, whatever possessed you? My dearest darling love, my Ellie."

Doc glanced at Wallace. He was grinning like an ape, pointing at Titus, tittering. Doc slapped him hard, snapping his head back.

"What the hell you do that for?"

"Get over in the corner, you garbage, out of my sight!"

Titus continued holding her body like a mother holding an infant, sitting rocking back and forth, ignoring, the blood patching his shirt at the shoulder and starting down his sleeve.

Raider and Algernon ran crouching, keeping close to the buildings.

It was so dark the Englishman couldn't see Raider five feet ahead of him. Up top, Florry-Mae and her girl friends were keeping the defenders busy, pouring brief volleys into the upstairs windows of the general store and at the corners of buildings and other likely posts for sharpshooters.

"You don't even know where you're going," rasped Algernon irritably.

"I don't know where Doc and that banker are, either," responded Raider. "It's so dark down here you can't even tell one building from another. And we could find six-guns waiting for us round the next corner. Why don't you tell me something I don't know? All I do know is that they're down here. Hold it!''

Algernon ran into his outstretched hand, reacting, recoiling at the contact, and, for the first time in their association, cursing.

''You son of a bitch, don't do that!''

Raider laughed lightly. ''Hey, that's good, you're finally learning English. Look over there, that line o' light under that shade. Notice anything peculiar about it?''

''It's the only light on that side of the street.''

''Good eye, mister. That's where they are, they got to be.''

''You have no way in Christendom of knowing for certain.''

''They are. Come on.''

They crossed the street, in doing so placing themselves in the line of fire. A shot from above whistled by Raider's ear, splintering a roof post close by.

''Jesus! How in hell can they see?''

He froze in his tracks. The light inside the bank had gone out. The door slammed open, a single shot cracking between him and Algernon, singing Raider's sleeve.

''Hold it right there!''

''Doc!'' thundered Raider.

''You heard me. . . . Great God! Is that you, Rade?''

''What the hell you mean letting go close up like that? You coulda blown my elbow clear across the street. Don't you look to see what you're shooting at before you pull?''

''It's Raider, all right,'' said Doc back over his shoulder.

Raider and Algernon hurtled inside. Doc slammed the door. He relit the lamp, holding it up. Raider gaped, pointing at Wallace.

''It's him!''

''Jasper Wilke–Hobart–Donaldson, whatever your real name is, you are to consider yourself taken in charge.'' Algernon clapped a hand on Wallace's shoulder.

Raider's eyes strayed to Titus, who continued to cradle his wife in his arms.

''Ellie, Ellie.''

Doc shook his head. "It's a long story, Rade. I'll fill you in on all the details later." He flung one hand toward the vault. "There's better than a million in cash in there. But see here, how in the devil did you find us?"

"Eustace."

"He's dead." Doc hung his head and shook it slowly.

"The hell he is. He's live as you are. Fulla holes, maybe, but on the mend. Ain't that so, Algernon?"

"He's being treated by a physician for multiple wounds, but he's doing famous'y. He'll recover. We found him out on the plain and brought him back to Blacktower."

"That's good news."

"Getting real palsy with him, eh?" murmured Raider, a tinge of envy in his tone.

"I like Eustace. He grows on you. You'd like him. Everybody does."

"Except the two who put the five slugs into him." Raider looked about. "We got to get outta here, Doc. Florry-Mae and a bunch up top are keeping the bastards busy. Let's haul before they run outta ammo."

Raider turned his attention to tying Wallace's hands behind his back, using the money sack drawcords.

"This boy's our ticket outta here," he said to Doc.

"Don't count too heavily on him. Just about everybody out there except his brother would love to see him dead and wouldn't hesitate to do the honors."

"What do you think's the best way outta here?" Raider asked him.

Doc rubbed his chin reflectively. "I guess the way you came in. There's no secret passage through the hills, if that's what you're looking for. If only there was some way to distract them."

"I have an idea," said Algernon. He extended his hand to Doc. "I say, I don't believe we've been introduced. Braithwaite's the name, Algernon Gerald Braithwaite."

"Doc Weatherbee. Delighted to make your acquaintance, I'm sure."

"Delighted to make *yours*. Do my ears deceive me, or do you actually speak proper English?"

"Cut the shit, Algernon!" exclaimed Raider. "What's this big idea you got?"

Algernon suggested that all of them stay put for a few minutes. He would "venture forth" carrying the lamp. Go straight to the general store and toss it in through a window. Within two minutes the entire store, containing at least half the defenders, would be ablaze.

"It will provide the perfect distraction," he chortled, rubbing his hands briskly, completely taken with his idea.

"Only if you put the thing clean through the window," said Raider.

"Not to worry, old chap. It happens I'm a champion bowler at cricket. At the range I'll be throwing I can't possibly miss."

"What do you think, Doc?" Raider asked.

"Do it, Algernon." Doc eased open the door for him, Seizing the lamp, Algernon turned the flame down and went out.

"I'll take the little shit," said Raider to Doc. He glanced back at Titus, holding the body of his wife. Doc crossed over to the banker.

"Erland, we're leaving now. Erland . . ."

"Ellie."

"Erland."

Doc tried to loosen Titus's hold, but he stiffened, glaring at him balefully, then resumed his rocking.

"Leave him," said Raider.

"He's crazier than a coot," piped Wallace.

They ignored him. Raider glanced out the open door into the darkness. The tiny dot of light, the lamp wick, was moving diagonally across the street in the direction of the store, floating like a will-o'-the-wisp, Algernon totally obscured by the blackness.

Doc joined Raider in the doorway. "I'm getting a chilling thought," he said soberly. "What if the sound of the glass breaking brings someone running fast enough to put the fire out before it really gets going?"

Raider watched the dot of light lift upward as Algernon

mounted the steps. It moved to the left and began dancing crazily. Then came the faint sound of shattering glass.

"I think he's worried about the same thing, Doc. Look at the light, the son of a bitch is climbing through the window. What guts!"

The light vanished. Seconds later the window framed leaping flames. Smoke billowed forth into the night.

"Where in hell did he get to?" Worry furrowed Raider's brow. He bit his lower lip and drew in his breath sharply.

Algernon came pounding up. "Don't just stand there, let's go!"

Doc cast a last look at Erland. Then he went to him again and tried to pull him to his feet, but the banker resisted, clinging tightly to the body. Raider pulled Doc away.

"Leave him. They won't hurt him. They got enough to do worrying 'bout their own hides."

Pushing Wallace ahead of him, his .45 planted in the small of his back, Raider followed Doc and Algernon down the street, retracing the route he and the Englishman had come in by. By now the store was an inferno. Enormous tongues of flame leaped from the side windows, and the roof of a smaller building next door caught fire, the dried shakes going up like tinder.

They rushed up into the hills, Wallace stumbling, Raider's gun jabbing at his spine, straightening him. Up to the top they climbed, the store now solid flame, igniting the buildings both right and left of it. By the firelight Raider could see men running about in panic. The guns rimming the hilltops spoke sporadically. One outlaw after another caught lead and died.

"That was the best goddamn idea you ever had!" bellowed Raider to Algernon. "You climbed in the window. What in hell did you light that went up so fast?"

"What didn't I? Everything in sight with a tin of benzine spilled all about the place. I bloody well singed my eyebrows."

"Good man," said Doc.

Algernon nodded. "I fancy so."

Raider rolled his eyes at Doc.

"It's murder!" blurted Wallace. "Coldest-blooded ever. You caught them boys like rats in a trap, you heartless, goddamn son—"

Algernon had whirled on him. Cocking his right, he slammed him full in the face, knocking him cold and setting his nose bleeding again.

"Goooooood man," said Doc.

CHAPTER EIGHTEEN

Two of Florry-Mae's Volunteers, as Doc promptly dubbed them, suffered serious injuries. Angela died of her wounds. Zora had taken a bullet in the hand, in the meat of her thumb, and a shot had found its way through her right rib cage. Had it entered the opposite side it would have stopped her heart; nevertheless, it was painful, and Doc and Algernon agreed that it had entered the lung. Raider and Algernon got her back to town as fast as they could. They also brought in four prisoners in addition to Wallace. Ben Hungerford was dead, shot in the back. Before leaving to return to Blacktower, Doc went looking for Erland Titus. He wasn't in the bank. Doc searched the town, but failed to locate him. He decided to remain behind to look further.

Arriving in Blacktower, Algernon carried the wounded Zora up the steps to Reichert's office. A light was still burning in the window, despite the fact that it was well past midnight. Florry-Mae walked ahead of Algernon and opened the door. They found Reichert standing in the center of the office, his wizened face black with anger. The place was a shambles, broken bottles, a chair overturned, the corner cot upended, the bedding scattered about. On the table lay Eustace. The sheet had been drawn up to cover his face. Florry-Mae took one look, the horror of the sight registered, and she screamed. Algernon followed her inside, carrying Zora, who was moaning softly. Florry-Mae raced to the table. Reichert stepped in front of her just as she was about to lift the sheet.

"No!"

He grabbed her wrists, pushing her backwards.

"Put that one in the stuffed chair," he said, nodding at Algernon.

"I'm afraid she's been shot in the lung."

"Mmmmm."

"What happened? *What happened!*" screamed Florry-Mae.

"Quiet down, damn it. Get hold of yourself. We . . . I lost him. I'm sorry. I couldn't stop the bleeding. God knows I tried. I did everything I could. He was doing fine, splendidly, taking nourishment, gabbing away, talking coherently. His color was coming back beautifully. His fever was down, his pain under control. I doped him up, you see," he said, appealing for understanding from Algernon. "I was feeding him broth. He choked. Terribly. Wrenching. He couldn't stop choking. He started bleeding internally. Bleeding, bleeding, the life seeping out of him. I couldn't stop it. I couldn't do a thing." He paused, shifting his eyes to Florry-Mae. He laughed, a near-hysterical cackling. "It's crazy. Insane. He was so strong. I took five bullets out of him. He survived. Strong as an ox. He was coming along beautifully. That damned broth. He choked. Oh, little girl, little girl, I couldn't help him. Don't you understand, I couldn't."

He tore his eyes from her, releasing her wrists, grabbing a bottle from the table at his elbow, smashing it against the wall. "I'm so sorry, so sorry . . ."

Florry-Mae had gone deathly pale, her lower lip quivering, her eyes riveted to the body, the sheet completely covering it. A slender line of blood showed through it—the bandage across Eustace's chest, saturated, soaked through. She opened and closed her hands rapidly, nervously as she walked slowly toward the table, reaching it, bending over it, embracing him.

"Eustace, Eustace. I love you, love you. Eustace . . ."

The sun was rising, fiery red, painting the eastern sky amethyst. Doc had searched the town, finding two blackened bodies in the rubble of the general store and others strewn about the area. But there was no sign of either

Titus. Two buildings Doc could not get into; the doors to both were locked, their windows boarded. One was the saloon; the other, a church standing at the far end of the street, its foundation clustered with weeds, its steps broken, the left-hand railing lying on the ground, as if it had been lassoed and pulled from its place. The belfry balanced on the ridgepole was open on four sides, its bell missing. Two starlings cavorted about it as Doc approached the church a second time. The birds trilled musically, brightly welcoming him, the sunlight painting their plummage in a rainbow of colors.

He picked his way up the broken steps. Again he tried the double front door, throwing his shoulder against first one side, then the other. They stood firm, but there was a quarter inch gap between them. Getting out his penknife, he pushed the blade through the crack, lifting the inner latch. With his left hand he pushed open one door.

The interior was barren of pews or benches. The carelessly boarded windows admitted slender bands of sunlight. The ceiling rose, lifting to the base of the belfry. On the altar was a podium, behind it a table positioned horizontally. A musty odor filled the place. Cobwebs stretched across every corner and under the windowsills.

Seated on a bench at the head of the aisle was Titus, holding the corpse of his wife beside him, his right arm firmly about her shoulder, her head lolling against his shoulder.

"Erland."

No response. The breeze whistled eerily through the belfry overhead. Doc started up the aisle. It wasn't until he got to them and was able to look down over their shoulders that he saw the dandelions, yellow clover, and some kind of orange-red flowers in her lap. Titus was holding her wedding ring, preparing to push it onto her finger. Doc sighed mutely and touched Titus's shoulder.

"Erland."

He turned. "Shhhh," he whispered. "You're interrupting the ceremony. Please, take your seat with the others."

Doc nodded and stepped back a few paces, moving to

his right. He looked across at Titus. He was mumbling, slipping the ring onto her finger, turning, and kissing her. Then, still supporting her with his right hand, he lifted her in his arms as if she were light as a feather, taking care not to spill any of the flowers from her lap. He turned and carried her up the aisle. Doc followed. At the door Titus staggered; Doc caught hold of her, taking her from him.

Titus was smiling. A strange, mystical tranquility had settled over him. He appeared completely relaxed, perfectly content.

But in his eyes was madness.

"Open the door, Erland."

Titus stared through him, his smile broadening. Then, abruptly, confusion seized him, pinching his brows together, narrowing his eyes, bending the corners of his thin-lipped mouth downward. A single tear formed on the lower lid of his left eye. It grew larger and started down his cheek.

"Open the door," Doc repeated.

Titus jerked his head, snapping to attention, nodding, opening the door. He started down the steps. Reaching the ground, he began hurrying his step.

"Wait," called Doc.

Titus paid no attention. He broke into a run, suddenly filled with strength, completely oblivious of his wounds. Up the street he ran, turning into the bank, slamming the door in his wake. Doc followed. His burden was getting heavier with every step. He stumbled and nearly fell. Kneeling, he laid her down, regained his feet, and ran toward the bank. He was within ten feet of the closed door when a muffled shot sounded.

"Erland!"

He pushed open the door. Titus lay facedown on the floor, his right arm outstretched, in his grasp a nickel-plated revolver, smoke issuing ominously from the muzzle. The bullet had shattered his temple, crimsoning the side of his head; a shaft of sunshine spotlighted it, brightening the color.

"Erland, Erland," whispered Doc, crouching beside him. "Poor tortured man."

He looked around, found a pick and shovel, and went
back outside and dug a grave behind the church close by
the tiny cemetery overgrown with weeds, the two starlings
perched on the roof watching him curiously. He buried the
Tituses side by side, marking the grave with a rude cross
fashioned of two loose boards fastened together with a
single nail. He scattered the wildflowers Erland had picked
and placed in Ellie's lap over the mound of earth. Lines
from Corinthians came to mind. They seemed appropriate.
He stood at the foot of the grave, his head bowed reverently.

"For what knowest thou, O wife, whether thou shalt
save thy husband? or how knowest thou, O man, whether
thou shalt save thy wife?"

In the hereafter, he might have added, he reflected. The
unknown and the unknowable; they do so dominate the
lives of us all.

He walked around to the front of the church to take one
last look at the town—the Russian thistle tumbling about
the street, the weeds and grasses clinging resolutely to life
in the now broiling sun, the charred rubble of the general
store, black reminder of the bloodshed of the previous
night, the starlings returned to the vacant belfry and flitting
about—and he reflected on the legion of nameless ghosts
destined to remain in this place for all eternity.

Mounting his horse, he rode away. Halfway up into the
hills he noticed the bulge in his pocket. Reining up, he
brought out the gun with which Titus had taken his life. It
was small, .22 caliber, the sort of toy a woman would
carry in a specially tailored pocket holster. Particularly a
beautiful woman, one vulnerable to undesired attention
and admiration.

CHAPTER NINETEEN

When Doc returned to Blacktower it was to the stunning disclosure that Eustace was dead. Raider informed him; Doc's anger mounted to a pitch of fury as he listened.

"You two said he was fine. On the mend. He'll recover!"

"He was doing very well when we left," said Algernon sheepishly.

They stood in front of the marshal's office. Raider and Algernon had been awaiting Doc's return, scanning the horizon, looking for his horse. The news crushed him; he was furious. Which surprised Raider. In all their years together he had never seen his partner—former partner—take the death of a friend so hard. Had he himself been a stranger to the situation and those involved, he would have immediately assumed that Doc and Eustace were father and son.

Eustace was buried in Blacktower. The entire town turned out in acknowledgment of his heroism and to display the sympathy one and all felt for Florry-Mae in her hour of pain. The prisoners had been turned over to Marshal Huggens, who had come back from Elkins with his deputies. The money recovered was placed in the local bank to await certification of claims upon it by the banks, express offices, and individuals from whom it had been stolen. Word of Wallace Hungerford's capture spread eastward to the Oklahoma Panhandle and the sites of his earlier crimes. That hanging was too good for him went without saying in the views of those familiar with his bloodthirsty exploits, but since the law could prescribe no harsher punishment, it appeared certain that he would be tried, convicted, and hanged.

A tearful and subdued Florry-Mae, attired in widow's weeds, met with Raider, Doc, and Algernon on the verandah of the Hotel Blodgett as the three Pinkertons prepared to leave for Kansas City and reassignment.

Doc held Florry-Mae's hands fondly, looking deep into her eyes, which were reddened from almost continuous crying.

"I have to get this off my chest," he said. "Back in Old Blacktower, when he smacked those two misfits and got away, if I'd had my wits about me, if it all hadn't happened so damned fast, I would have stopped him."

"You wouldn't have. He was twice your size. They couldn't stop him, and you wouldn't have been able to. Besides, if he hadn't got away, Mr. Raider and Mr. Braithwaite would never have found him and brought him in. I'd never have gone to Dr. Reichert's office. They'd never have known you were a prisoner out there."

"She's right, Doc," said Raider solemnly.

Doc nodded reluctantly. "I guess. Still, I can't help feeling rotten about it. I was responsible for him."

"Uncle Doc," said Florry-Mae, cupping his cheek in one gloved hand, striving to smile, and only partially succeeding.

"He was a fine boy, Florry-Mae. A jewel. He had a heart as big as a barn door. I'll never forget him, never."

"You're getting tears in your eyes," she said, peering into them.

"Nonsense, I never cry. I don't know how."

Raider snickered. She looked from one to the next appealingly. Algernon appeared to be getting restless, she noted. He didn't know what to do with his hands and he kept looking off in the direction they would be traveling.

"I know you have to leave," she said, "but will you come back and see us sometime?"

"One of us'll have to," said Raider. "Got to testify against that little wart." He glanced at Algernon. "Me, more'n likely."

"I'll be back," said Doc. "I give you my word I will."

"I'll stand both o' you drinks at Poindexter's. Look."

She pointed across the street and up the block. The crossed boards and closed sign had been removed from the front of Poindexter's. The inside night door was open. The batwing doors beckoned invitingly.

"I shall stand everybody drinks," announced Algernon brightly. "Now. I don't know about you three, but I'm thirsty as a Mongol in the Gobi."

"I can't go in wearing black," said Florry-Mae. "Wouldn't be right. When you come back we'll drink."

She threw her arms around their necks, one after another, pulling them down, kissing them affectionately. Doc was last.

"You take care of yourself, Uncle Doc."

"Always. I'm much too valuable to the agency to take unnecessary chances with my person."

"Oh, Chrissakes," sputtered Raider, waving away the suggestion with both hands. "Let's go, we got to be a good ways from here before sundown. We got us close to eight hundred miles to go. You can do your drinkin' from your canteen, Algernon."

Doc climbed up on his wagon seat. Raider and Algernon mounted their horses.

"You planning to drive poor Judith all the way to Kansas City?" asked Florry-Mae.

"No. We're heading up the line to Tucumcari, said Raider. We'll board the Chicago, Rock Island & Pacific up there. Pinkertons ride most rails free, Florry-Mae, even Judith. It's one of the few fringe benefits the agency offers."

They rode away. She stood in the middle of the street waving good-bye until distance reduced her to a speck behind them.

"Poor little girl," said Raider.

"Poor everyone," said Algernon. "What a bloodthirsty country. It's positively execrable."

"Isn't it, though?"

•   •   •

Raider and Algernon sat staring out the window, watching the sere, yellow, and unrelievedly flat landscape of south-central Kansas slip by. The car hung heavy with cigar smoke, a condition distasteful to Raider, one which invariably played hob with his sensitive stomach. The whistle hooted, smoke billowed past the grimy window, momentarily obscuring the view, and cinders sprayed over the ditch alongside the tracks. Upwards of twenty passengers shared the car with them, including a dignified-looking elderly man sporting a fundamentalist beard and a beaver that looked as if a small herd had trampled it; a large woman wrapped in pink silk embroidered with lace proudly displaying hideously crimsoned lips under a huge nose centering a sowlike face; and five seedily dressed young men who looked like brothers and were engaged in a spirited game of twenty-one.

"It's been quite an experience, hasn't it?" said Algernon in a tone that suggested he craved conversation, even argument—anything to shatter the bastion of boredom silence was building around them.

"Yeah, quite." Raider turned in his seat to look down the aisle. "What's he up to? He's been back there twenty minutes." He got up. "Hold the fort, I'm going back and see."

He ambled down the aisle, the jerking train sending him against one seat, then another alternately all the way to the vestibule. He eased aside the lazytongs gate and entered the car behind. It was a freight car pressed into temporary service as a rolling stable. His own horse and Algernon's stood head to head, as if they were holding a conversation. At the far end he could see Doc busy brushing down Judith.

" 'lo, Rade. What's the matter, getting bored looking at Kansas?"

"Just wanted to stretch my legs."

He ran his hand down Judith's mane. She whinnied softly, clomping one hoof.

"I think she's lonesome," said Doc. "She's the only mule in here."

"She sure musta missed you when you were holed up out there with the boy." Raider cleared his throat self-consciously. "I been meaning to tell you, Doc, I'm real sorry what happened happened. I didn't get to know him very good, but he seemed like a good soul. He was tougher'n a turkey buzzard."

"Just not tough enough, eh?" Doc sighed heavily. "Billy Pinkerton and Eustace's uncle are going to hang my hide on a nail when they hear about it. The chief'll probably come after me with a bullwhip."

"It wasn't your fault."

"He's dead, Rade, and I was supposed to look out for him."

"You make it sound like he was in swaddling clothes."

"In a sense he was. Green as grass. By God, this is the end of our stick I really despise. The bloody part. Every time I think of poor Florry-Mae . . ."

"She's young, she'll get over it."

"What the hell does age have to do with it?"

"Now, don't go starting up, I didn't mean nothing."

"I know. I'm sorry, I'm just edgy."

"Worried about the big bosses."

"To hell with the big bosses! I just . . . Losing him is like . . . Oh hell, let's forget it. Let's keep it out of the conversation from here on."

"Kinda sad about Titus and his missus."

"I'll say. Tragic. Still, if you think about it, it's the only way it could have ended for them. Erland never could have gone on without her. When we were locked up together he told me that when she first ran off he nearly went out of his mind. But by sheer force of will he blocked her out. Threw himself into his work and tried his level best to forget her. Only then they came back and robbed him, and he knew she was involved, knew she'd duplicated his key before she deserted him. He always kept it in one corner of the drawer. When he went looking for it it was there, all right, but not where he'd placed it. When they hit the bank, getting in with a key the way they did, he put two and two together."

"His mistake was going looking for her."

"He was mad, Rade. All of a sudden he stopped moping and fantasizing and blew up. He went after her to find her and her friends and bring them in. Only, when he finally caught up with her, the mere sight of her was enough to cool him down and turn him to jelly. He worshiped her."

"A body should never let himself get that smitten with any woman."

"That's easy to say." He finished brushing Judith down. "Little girl's a trifle nervous. I don't think she relishes being cooped up with all these horses."

Raider drew a deep breath through his nose and made a face. "It ain't the horses, it's the horseshit. How in hell do you stand the stink all closed in like this?"

"They sweep out every night after supper."

"You 'bout done here?"

"All done."

He nuzzled Judith's ear, talking in low, confidential tones to her, kissed her, raising Raider's eyes in their sockets, and the two of them started back.

"Where you figure they'll send you next, now that this business is all wrapped up?" Raider asked.

"That's a dumb question. How am I supposed to know? How about you?"

"Yeah, it's dumb."

They crossed over the coupling into the passenger car in silence, each preoccupied with his own thoughts. Each one had missed working with the other, each had been elated when their respective assignments had eventually brought them together, each wanted to mention in passing how pleased he had been that that had come about.

But neither said a word about it.

Doc changed the subject of his thoughts as they started up the aisle, Raider preceding him.

"You like working with Braithwaite?"

"Oh yeah, sure, he's aces. Savvy as hell. All kinds of education. Catches onto things real fast. Great with a gun, too. Sure knows how to handle himself with people."

"Is he staying in this country?"

"Yeah."

"So you'll still be working together."

"Far as I know. Why?"

"Just curious."

"You'd like him, Doc. He's a regular prince."

"He seems nice."

"You'll be getting a new sidekick, right?"

"I expect." Doc cleared his throat, announcing their arrival to Algernon, who was sitting with his back to them, writing in the case journal. "Hello again."

Algernon turned and smiled. "How's Judith?"

"Okay."

They took their seats across from him. He went back to his writing. Raider leaned against the window post, folded his arms, set his feet on the empty seat across from Doc, and, tilting down his Stetson, fell asleep under it, snoring softly. Doc eyed him, grunted, and returned to the safe and cheerless privacy of his thoughts.

CHAPTER TWENTY

The bar in the Oak Room of the Hotel Independence flanked one entire wall, running not two inches under eighty feet, in Raider's estimation. No fewer than six bartenders attired in bright red Cossack jackets with gold roping and piping and gleaming brass buttons bobbed and twisted, poured and mixed and wiped, and rang the six cash registers at their backs under a ten-panel mirror that looked to Raider like the Erie Canal laid on its side. The foot rail shone golden. He hesitated to step on it for fear of smudging it with the mud of New Mexico still clinging to the inside of his heels.

Organized bedlam reigned—hearty laughter, booming voices, and smoke rising to the mauve and gold-leaf ceiling crisscrossed with stout oaken beams—as he, Algernon, and Doc stepped up to the bar. Four massive chandeliers suspended from chains whose links were two inches thick illuminated the windowless room, sheening the highly polished paneling enclosing the mass dismissal of thirst.

Raider felt out of place. He cast an envious eye first at Doc, then at Algernon. Both were impeccably attired: Doc wore a newly acquired wool cheviot walking suit with a gold and black domino vest, his favorite pearl stickpin, and imported English shoes sporting a gleam calculated to set anyone glancing at them blinking; Algernon was decked out in a slate gray Russian linen ensemble over a matching vest over an expensive cotton shirt topped by a black-figured silk four-in-hand tie. Raider felt out of place, despite the fact that he had exhibited sufficient presence of mind to remove his Stetson upon entering the lobby and had taken pains to shave in the men's room at the railroad station. The look in Doc's eye as he paused on the front steps before entering to assess Raider's attire warned him that a compliment would not be forthcoming. Doc had smiled and declared him to be "neat as a grizzly," prompting a loud and derisive laugh from Algernon.

"Clothes don't make the goddamn man, anyhow," Raider muttered, hoisting his whiskey, admitting a liberal quantity into his mouth, and letting it slide down his throat.

"What was that, old boy?" asked Algernon.

"Nothing."

Doc smirked. "He said clothes don't make the g.d. man. Of course they don't, Rade. All clothes do is make one look halfway presentable, respectable, civilized in an uncivilized world."

"Balls."

He glanced up at the outsized Sedan clock set half in the fifth mirror panel, half in the sixth. The hands read twenty minutes before four.

"Where the hell is Billy Pinkerton, do you think?"

"He'll be here," said Doc.

Algernon checked his Jurgenson watch against the clock and tsked in annoyance. "I say, my man." He snapped his fingers at the nearest bartender.

"Sir?"

"Your clock is approximately sixty-five seconds fast." He held his watch up.

The bartender stared in disbelief, at the same time backing off.

Algernon scowled. "I say."

"Algernon, for chrissakes, the man doesn't care."

"Well he bloody well ought to!"

A bellboy came marching through, his pillbox hat at a jaunty angle, one gloved hand supporting a silver tray, on it an envelope.

"Mr. Weatherbee, Mr. Braithwaite. Mr. Braithwaite, Mr. Weatherbee . . ."

"Here, son," said Doc, waving him over. He took the envelope. "Rade, give him a tip."

"Why me? You got the message."

Algernon laughed and tossed a quarter onto the tray.

"The walrus has arrived," said Doc wearily. "Ah me. Drink up, gentlemen, time to face the music."

Raider confessed to never having seen either plush seats or a chandelier in an elevator before. Reaching the fourth floor, they made their way down the carpeted corridor in the direction of 404. Standing before the door, Doc raised his fist to knock, then paused, looking first at Algernon, then Raider.

"Go ahead," said Raider. "You're holding up the works. He's not hauling us on the carpet. It's your show."

"Bless you, plowboy."

William Pinkerton greeted them, his walrus mustache having added a half inch to each end since they had last seen him. His eyes as always suggested that he hadn't slept in two nights. He was in his shirt-sleeves, two-inch wide galluses climbing up and over his narrow shoulders, his bow tie loosened and awry. His suitcase lay on the bed, opened but not yet unpacked.

They shook hands all around. "Braithwaite," he said, moving to the bed and producing a sand-colored envelope from the pocket of his jacket, which lay at the foot. "This came just before I left Chicago."

"Excuse me, all," murmured Algernon. He perused the cablegram. "It's from my superiors. I'm to contact them at once. Would you excuse me, Mr. Pinkerton?"

"Sure. I think you can write out a cablegram down at the front desk. They'll see that it gets on the wire."

Algernon left. Pinkerton looked first at Raider, then at Doc. He got a half bottle of rye out of his suitcase and a tumbler from the bathroom.

"Only one glass. Hope you don't mind passing it around." He poured. "So your paths crossed, did they?"

"Just at the windup," said Raider.

"Eustace Hillbank was killed."

His tone was not accusing. He was merely stating a fact, Raider noted. Doc looked relieved, the tautness going out of his face.

"We were captured," he said. "They were putting us in a cell. Eustace jumped the two of them, and in the hullabaloo that followed, he got away."

Pinkerton nodded. "Only they caught up with him later and shot him."

"We found him and brought him in," said Raider. "The doc who worked on him did a fine job. He died accidental, choking on broth. It started him bleeding inside. The doc couldn't stop it. Freakiest thing you ever saw."

"So it seems. Unfortunately, *how* he died is of little interest to his parents and his Uncle William. He was only eighteen."

"I know that, damn it!" exclaimed Doc. "I know it, and I've got to live with it, all of it. Get it off your chest, Billy. Read me the damned riot act and get it over with. We've got other things to talk about!"

Raider laid a consoling hand on Doc's shoulder; the smaller man shook it off irritably, swinging about and stomping off into the other room. He slammed the door so loudly a bit of plaster loosed itself from the molding and dropped to the floor.

"He took it real hard," said Raider quietly. "He'd come to love the boy like his own son. When he found out what happened—I mean all of us figured Eustace was on the mend, and he was. When Doc found out, when he got back to Blacktower and I told him, I thought he was going into shock. His face got all red, his eyes bulged out. It couldn'ta hit him harder than if it had been his own flesh and blood."

Pinkerton nodded. "I'm sure."

"If old man Wagner is going to give him hell . . ."

"He's not. Don't worry about it. I'll take care of everything at the other end."

"That'd be real decent of you, Bill."

"Mmmmm. Well, drink up, drink up. We've still got an inch in the bottom."

"I've had my fill, thanks."

Pinkerton poured and drank and sat at the foot of the bed. "How did you and Braithwaite get along out there?"

"Oh, just great."

"No friction?"

"Not really."

"Not really. What does that mean? I mean, let's be honest—he's English and you're Arkansas. You must have rubbed each other the wrong way once in a while."

"Maybe a little, nothing serious."

"You think he learned anything?"

"I guess."

"Did you?"

Raider shrugged. "You want to ask me one special question? I mean to say, is that the bush all this beating about is about?"

"Do you think he'd like to go out with you again?"

"Hadn't you best ask him?"

"Would you go out with him?"

"I guess."

"Just the suggestion gets you all worked up, I see."

"What the hell you want me to do, jump up and down?"

"I suspect you may not get the opportunity. I've a hunch that cable he got is from his people back at Scotland Yard calling him home. In the event he does leave, you'll be needing a new partner again. Any thoughts?"

"Isn't making up the love matches your department?"

"I don't suppose you'd consider teaming up with Weatherbee again."

"I haven't thought about it."

"Think about it. What do you say?"

"I say it's up to him. He's the one broke us up in the first place."

"That's not exactly the way I remember it, but we'll let it pass."

A knock sounded. Algernon came back in waving the cablegram. "Friends, Romans, lend me your ears. I regret to say that my delightful stay in your delightful country has come to its end. I've been ordered to return to London posthaste. I've sent word on ahead to expect me."

Listening to him, watching him, Raider's impression

was that he was overjoyed but striving to be lighthearted, tossing it off.

"That's a shame," said Pinkerton. "We'll certainly miss you. Raider here was just saying what a great job you did. How he would have been lost without you. Isn't that so, Raider?"

"Wha . . .? Oh, yeah, sure."

"He's exaggerating, Mr. Pinkerton. He's the one deserving of the kudos. Well, gentlemen, it's been marvelous, an experience I shall never forget. I loathe good-byes." He glanced about. "Where's Weatherbee?"

Raider tilted his head toward the inner door. "Nature called."

"Oh dear. Well, say good-bye for me, there's a good chap." He extended his hand and shook Raider's, then Pinkerton's. "I shall drop the case journal off on my way out. It's in my saddlebags in temporary storage. Ta ta!" He waved and was gone.

"Ta ta," said Raider to the closed door.

The inner door opened. Doc stood glaring.

"Raider," said Pinkerton, "why don't you give Braithwaite a hand. Run on downstairs with him and get the journal. So he won't have to bother coming all the way back up here. There's a good chap." He laughed.

Raider threw him a jaundiced look and left.

"Doc," began Pinkerton, "I know you're upset."

"Let's both just forget it, shall we? I'm a little loosely strung lately. Still, I shouldn't have mouthed off. I apologize."

"There's no need. Sit, there's something else you and I have to discuss. You're without a partner now, and your next assignment could come through any time. We're going to have to team you up with somebody. Any suggestions?"

"I'll leave it to you."

"No preference? No old hand you've had a hankering to work with?"

"No one special."

"Want to finish off what's left in the bottle?"

"No thanks."

"I don't suppose you'd consider teaming up with Raider again."

"I haven't thought about it."

"What do you think?"

"It's up to him. We never would have been separated in the first place if he wasn't so touchy. That's his big trouble, he can't take a simple joke."

"As I recall, what he couldn't take was you flirting with his lady."

"As *I* recall, she was the one doing the flirting."

"And you both wound up owing eleven hundred for damages plus interest. It's all so incredibly ridiculous. You two make far and away the best team in the agency." Doc lifted his head and put on a face of mock astonishment. "One of the best. Still, the finest oil and the purest water don't mix. If you can't get along, and you've certainly proven you can't . . ."

"I wouldn't say that," said Doc.

"No?"

"You've got to understand something. We're not a couple of figure filberts or ribbon clerks. This isn't the safest, cushiest, most relaxing job in the world. We operate under a lot of pressure."

"I agree."

"We wouldn't be human if we didn't snap at each other once in a while."

"Then it's agreed, you and Raider will resume working together."

"I didn't agree to that. You're putting words in my mouth."

"How about if I ask him?"

"I think you'd better."

"What would you say if I told you I already have. And he's all for it."

"Who are you kidding? Raider said that?"

"On my word of honor. How do you feel about it? What do I tell him?"

"Well, if he thinks he's going to make me the heavy,

put the black hat on my head, he's got another think coming!''

"Why don't I tell him the truth—that I tried, but you're just not interested.''

"Wait, wait, I didn't say that.''

"Then what?''

A knock. Pinkerton sighed in exasperation. Raider came back in, the case journal under his arm.

"Doc, you okay?''

"Raider, he's agreed that you two should get back together as a team.''

"Hold everything!'' burst Doc.

"Hold nothing!'' burst Pinkerton. "I give up! The hell with it. You can team up with grizzly bears for all I care. I'm through pleading and cajoling. This isn't the sixth grade, and we're not trying to get together on who's going to be recess monitor. We're trying to run a business. We're playing for keeps. It may interest you to know that the chief doesn't want you back together. He thinks it'd be a horrendous mistake. He suggested we put six states between you on your next assignments so your paths can't possibly cross. My brother Robert feels the same way, and so does Bill Wagner. I'm the damned fool who thought it made sense to pair you up again.''

Doc and Raider exchanged glances.

"I'm through talking. You can do as you damned well please!''

"There,'' began Doc.

"What?''

"I was just going to say there must be some way we can resolve this. If he's willing, if he says he is, I'll go along.''

"No you don't!'' snapped Raider. "He's got to say it first, Bill.''

"Shut your mouths, both of you.'' Pinkerton dug in his watch pocket. "There's only one way to settle it. I'm going to toss this nickel. Heads you team up again, tails you don't and never will. Fair enough?''

Both nodded hesitantly, each of them avoiding the other's

eyes. The coin was tossed. Pinkerton missed catching it; it landed on edge, rolling under the bed. He threw himself down, clapping his hand flat upon it.

"Watch me close. I'm not looking, I'm not turning it over, I'm just sliding it out. Here we are. What do you see?"

"Heads," muttered Raider.

"So it's settled. Now get out of here, both of you. I've got to unpack."

CHAPTER TWENTY-ONE

ALLAN PINKERTON, CHIEF
PINKERTON NATIONAL DETECTIVE AGENCY
191-193 FIFTH AVENUE
CHICAGO, ILLINOIS

PROBLEM OPERATIVES FINALLY RESOLVED SATISFAC-
TORILY STOP CONGRATULATIONS DUE YOU STOP
EMINENTLY CORRECT ANALYSIS SITUATION SUG-
GESTED MEASURES TO SOLVE SAME STOP TEAMING
EACH UP WITH OTHER PARTNERS IMPRESSED BOTH
HOW WELL OFF THEY WERE TOGETHER STOP TWO-
HEADED COIN YOU ADVISED PURCHASING HELPFUL
STOP AM RETURNING HOME TOMORROW ARRIVING
602 STOP ADVISE ROBERT HAVE OBTAINED HAND-
WORKED BELT WITH BRASS BUCKLE HE HAS SO LONG
COVETED STOP LOVE TO MOTHER STOP TRUST YOU
ARE IMPROVING EVERY DAY

WP

CHAPTER TWENTY-TWO

Raider stood at the bar watching the minute hand on the Sedan clock imbedded in the mirror in front of him click down to a quarter past one. Doc was fifteen minutes late. What, he wondered, could be detaining him? He sipped his Brotherhood Whiskey and water and chuckled softly to himself. Bill Pinkerton was a card, all right; a two-headed nickel, of all things. It had to have had two heads; why else would he keep it in his watch pocket separate from his change? And why hadn't he shown them both sides before flipping it, the way everybody does when they toss a coin? Yes sir, a real card. He laughed aloud; the men on either side of him stared; the bartender came over.

"May I help you, sir?"

"No."

"Rade."

Doc came pushing through the crowd to his rescue, waving a telegram.

"Where've you been? I been cooling my heels here since one."

"Had to wait for this. Just came from Chicago."

"Where do we go?"

"Back to Blackwater to testify, then to Montana."

"Oh boy, God's country."

"There's a range war brewing," said Doc, lowering his voice.

Raider groaned. "Let me see."

He reached for the telegram. Doc jerked it out of reach.
"It's just what I told you. Nothing else important."
"Let me see."
He snatched it from him and read:

. . . STOP SCHEDULE DEPARTURE ENABLE REACH
BLACKTOWER BY 15 STOP REGARDING CASES COM-
PLETED STOP AM APPRISED CIRCUMSTANCES TRAGIC
DEATH EH STOP HOLD W BLAMELESS THOUGH ADVISE IN
FUTURE MORE CAUTIOUS APPROACH DANGEROUS SIT-
UATIONS BETTER PROTECTIVE MEASURES FOR INEXPERI-
ENCED OPERATIVES STOP REGARDING MONIES OWED
BY YOU DAMAGES POLE CITY STOP 50 A MONTH AP-
PEARS INSUFFICIENT STOP SUGGEST ADDITIONAL SUM
NOT TO EXCEED 15 BE SUBTRACTED FROM EXPENSE
MONIES DUE YOU STOP OR MONTHLY SALARY CONTRI-
BUTION RAISED 10 STOP CHOICE YOURS STOP OFFICE
FORWARDING LIST YOUR QUESTIONABLE EXPENSE
CLAIMS STOP LIQUOR NOT PERMITTED UNDER EXPENSES
STOP HOW MANY TIMES MUST REMIND YOU SAME STOP
BLACKTOWER STABLE BOARDING FEE MULE WAGON
APPEARS EXORBITANT STOP SEPARATE HOTEL ROOMS
CONTRARY TRAVEL REGULATIONS STOP AGENCY NOT
RESPONSIBLE FOR REPLACING SHIRT TORN TO BANDAGE
WOUNDED STOP BANDAGES STANDARD TRAVEL SUPPLIES
STOP TRANSPORTATION WAGON KC UNNECESSARY IN
LIGHT FACT W RETURNING BLACKTOWER STOP REIM-
BURSEMENT LOSS W WINCHESTER INDIANS DENIED
STOP SITUATION APPEARS BADLY HANDLED REGARDING
SAME STOP SAME OBTAINS LOSS W DIAMONDBACK
PISTOL STOP MEAL ALLOWANCE 3 PER DIEM NOT 4
STOP ADJUSTMENT MADE ACCORDINGLY STOP ADVISE
DRASTICALLY CURTAIL DRINKING STOP MODERATE
IMBIBING ONLY UNDER SPECIAL CIRCUMSTANCES KNOWN
YOU STOP SUGGEST CEASE DRINKING ALTOGETHER
UNTIL POLE CITY DEBT SATISFIED STOP LIST 34 AD-
DITIONAL QUESTIONABLE EXPENSE ITEMS TO FOLLOW

STOP GOOD LUCK BOTH NEW ASSIGNMENT STOP KEEP
UP GOOD WORK

AP

"I'll drink to that," said Doc grandly, with a flamboy-
ant sweep of his hand. "How about you, Rade?"
"Bartender! Oh, bartender!"

J.D. HARDIN

**"THE MOST EXCITING
WESTERN WRITER SINCE
LOUIS L'AMOUR"
—JAKE LOGAN**